BE A MAN

^^^

16 Gay Erotic Stories

^^^

R. W. Clinger

Paxtonian Publishing
955 Bayridge Avenue
Pittsburgh, PA 15226

Be A Man: 16 Gay Erotic Stories
Copyright 2015 – R. W. Clinger

First Edition

1234567890

Made in the USA

Also by R. W. Clinger

~ ~ ~

For Kenito

Contents:

~ ~ ~

FIRST RESPONDER

~ ~ ~

"Rowdy? ... Rowdy, are you out there?"

Officer Kirk Rowdy, I believed, lifted the radio off his belt, pressed the CALL button, and replied in his deep and masculine voice, "Rowdy here."

I found out his frequency, acted like a cop at Station 782, and responded, "The Needly security alarm is going off again."

"A break-in with zone six, rear man-door area?"

"You got it ... Can you check it out?"

"I'm on it," Rowdy confirmed.

I imagined him clipping the radio to his belt again as he exited the coffee shop, slipping into his patrol car and zooming off for 625 Amsterton Drive (my house), a smile perched on his handsome face.

The West Hollywood abode was massive with its twenty-eight thousand square feet, pool and fountain in the back, two gardens, and a three car garage. I stared at Rowdy from a bedroom window as he drove around the confines. Rowdy, I assumed, didn't see anything out of the ordinary. No broken gates, no movement, and nothing questionable. He used the

4 digit pin number to the front iron gate, let himself in, and drove up to the entrance of the house.

The front door was open to the pitch black house, which caught Rowdy off guard at first. He looked for blood on the stoop, a broken lock, or damage to the door, but couldn't find any evidence of a break-in. Slowly he moved inside, was careful and on guard, and prepared for the most dangerous scenario of his life. He listened to interior sounds, my footsteps upstairs and water running. I imagined him carefully flicking on the foyer light, scanning the area, and proceeding throughout the still house. After lighting each room on the first floor, having found no sign of an emergency, he proceeded upstairs.

There was a band of yellow light at the top of the staircase from my bathroom. The sound of water spraying was louder there. Rowdy was familiar with the house, had visited there a few times before, but still advanced with caution. There, on the second floor he passed an empty office, two vacant but nicely decorated bedrooms, and located a subject of interest—light seeping out of my bathroom at the other end of the hall where I had slipped into a warm spray, and began to soap up my body.

I envisioned him creeping towards the light in a vigilant manner. Once reaching the other end of the hall, he stood outside the bathroom door, and watched secretly— obsessed.

Here was the star of the hour, Paul Needly in the shower. Rowdy saw my twenty-seven year old chiseled body with shiny blond hair, boy next door looks, plump lips, dark hazel eyes, hidden in the misty bathroom. He was out there beyond the steam, became excited and hard, all nine inches of meat swelled up in his blue uniform. Cautiously, Rowdy gazed into the tiny sliver of opened door and saw me soaping up my smooth looking chest, hairless pits, and strong thighs that were like vice grips. While lather circled nicely developed pecs and dripped down over a ladder-like chest, I observed Kirk Rowdy as he licked his lips, pressed his nine inch goods down into his navy slacks, fingered himself with a greedy hunger, ready for whatever came next. His stare concentrated on my seven inch cock dangling between firm legs as a waterfall dripped from its cut cap. Rowdy admired furry balls drooping behind the rod, smiled, craved the young actor, and desired me again … secretly.

In the shower's spray I smiled, became preoccupied with the soap and water, ran the white bar between my legs, up and along my rippled chest, and over succulent pecs. I pinched nipples and hardened my cock with greed. And accidentally, I dropped the bar of soap to the shower's stall, generously showed off my firm and bulbous ass to him, and eventually stood up with the bar of soap in hand. If I figured right, Officer Rowdy sported a woody the size of his Billy club, and caused himself to feel perturbed and uncomfortable, perhaps even conventionally perplexed by my solid body with its fit niceness. I smiled in the shadows of steam that enfolded my body, a necessary means of privacy between first responder and fresh actor. I gave Rowdy exactly what he wanted by rolling the bar of soap over my cock and balls, turned myself on, turned him on, and kept my goods hard with soapy suds that resembled guy-goo. Busy appendages worked beef and balls, pulled on skin and pushed on veins. Honestly, I was not really acting at all as I began to breathe heavily, overexcited with that one act play in my shower as chest rose and fell, as I spread my legs, ready for more action … only for the eyes of my delicious protector.

He was playing with himself out there, wasn't he? Could I not see his nine inch flag sticking out of his opened fly, a mass that was harder than hard with bristly cock-hair exposed? Did I not see his protrusion of man-staff that desired nothing less than his hands and fingers, or my mouth and throat, perhaps even my compressed and unyielding ass? I peered through the white mist inside the porcelain bathroom and saw him standing in the tiny crack that separated an officer of the law from a needy security alarm system owner, an actor with man-needs. Rowdy was working his goods like I was working mine. As fingers rushed up and down on his pole I found that he must have been overwhelmed with a feeling or need to burst a load on the outside of the door, accidentally coming, spraying cop goo everywhere ... just for me.

I groaned crazily as I rocked beef up and down, knowing that Rowdy was still out there, watching me as he licked his lips, unbuttoned the first three buttons on his shirt, exposed black chest hair and some of his solidly rippled abs, a left nipple and pec too. As pre-goo leaked out of my spigot I peered at the dimple in his chin, the coal colored sideburns on his butch and rough looking face that was ultimately handsome. He was sexy and trim, just right for my visual needs. Wickedly, I pumped my right hand as balls swung forward and almost touched the glass wall surrounding me. Emphatically, I moaned in the shower, ready and willed to blow my load, and was capable to perform for Officer Rowdy like he wanted me to, serving justice for man like a good citizen

The door swung open as I heard a mellow rhythm of masculine grunting. I blurted out, "Who's out there?" calling from inside the shower. "Who's there?" I sounded panicked and surprised, out of my mind. Quickly, I turned the spray off, pulled the shower curtain back, snatched up a towel and wrapped it around my body. I yelled with shock and terror, "Who's there? ... Tell me!" I bolted across the bathroom tile smelling like Ivory soap, needing to confront Rowdy.

I swung the door wide open and saw that the cop wasn't there in the hallway. He left me a surprise, though. On the hardwood floor was his navy uniform, sleek looking boots, a policeman's hat, and his musty boxer-briefs. I looked to the left and right, but didn't see him anywhere; the hallway was vacant. Seconds passed before I bent and picked up the white boxer-briefs, raised them to my mouth and nose, and inhaled their likable and rank aroma. Beneath the cotton towel, my rod bounced with new life. I was left to do

9

nothing more than treasure that moment, desiring Rowdy with simple elation, and became high and hard on his abandoned scent.

I moved down the hallway. In the dim, shifting light there were perilous drops of come leading the way, a man-trail for me to follow on the hardwood floors. Apparently, Rowdy had stroked himself free of a jizm-load, and had left me a pathway to track him. I was on his trail though, right behind him. He had made it downstairs, I believed, quickly taking the steps according to the droplets of spew that were discarded. I followed the trail with ease, and smiled hungrily. Accidentally the towel dropped from my waist because of a quick run while escaping the second floor. I rushed downstairs, still followed the cum-marks, and eventually ended up in my private study.

His naked, pumped, and rock-hard body was slumped on the couch. Officer Rowdy had his legs spread open as he toyed with his pounder by using both fists. The officer looked up from his work and smiled at me, soothingly said, "We have an intruder in the house, Needly."

I saw a bubble of pre-ooze at the tip of his cock. His firm legs glistened in the study's soft light. My eyes peered at his silken-hairy chest and a dimple in the center of his chin. I couldn't help myself, licked my lips, and merely stared at his moving palms on rod. I asked, "Did you check the grounds and all the rooms?"

"I think he got away. The dude's pretty coy … Apparently he took all your clothes away from you, Needly." His eyes strayed over my seven inches of flag, my glistening chest that was covered with warm spray, my solid pecs and V-shaped body, and hungrily smiled.

"My clothes?" I questioned.

"Forget about it, Needly. I'm here to protect you now. Why don't you come over here so I can make sure you're safe?"

I trusted him, desired him, and found him essential that evening. I was standing naked in the study, harder than hard, compulsive for his skin and touching, for our bodies to become one as man could willingly press into man. I moved towards him, cuddled between his legs, licked my lips, and found the nine inches of condom-covered staff protruding northward bound. On my knees, I leaned into the couch, smiled at him, and looked up the plane of his sculpted beauty. I began to lick the extra skin on his dangling balls, eventually placed the sack into my mouth, sucked repeatedly on the loose skin, and used my invited and warm tongue, pleasuring Kirk Rowdy to the fullest.

He ran fingers through my blond hair as I allowed his scrotum to fall out of my mouth. Impressively, I worked my lips and protruding tongue along the length of his veined shaft. I lapped at his stick with ease as his ball-hair brushed against my chin and cheeks. Rowdy's sack swung against my face in a romantically thrashing manner that caused my rod to bounce mysteriously and prosaically up and down.

And eventually, I slipped his uncut cockhead into my mouth, swallowed six inches of the mass, worked his protein along the back of my throat, up and down, and drove the pick into my insides. Rowdy started to moan above me, as if he was immediately hurt by the exposed intruder. I simply became lost beneath him, tasted plastic, gagged on him, smelled his musky aroma, took another inch of his cock into my mouth, fully attempted to plant the rod snugly between my lungs, and had it find my insides as its permanent harbor.

He couldn't take it, though. The cop was a trained killer. He was a skilled sharpshooter and rifleman, but he couldn't take my mouth-fixation as he thrust his hips upwards and into my throat, batted his rod into my hole, begged and pleaded beneath my suction to blow his load. Rowdy found my methods tantalizing and endless, charitable with a fierce movement and warmth—richly seductive. Officer Rowdy pushed my head away, cried above me, groaned and moaned, was unable to pent his load any longer. He was completely challenged by our connection, and was willing—at any moment—to shoot the liquid from his bat, becoming spent.

I understood his weakness and backed off. Above him, I stood with the hardest extension between my legs that I had ever felt, I said, "It's time for you to be like your name."

He smiled up at me, was glowing with a rough and rugged niceness. The cop was beyond handsome with his coal colored eyes, his exposed and uncut cock for my pleasure, his hairy chest, and dark sideburns that were nicely trimmed. He said, "You want to be rowdy, Needly?"

"Why do you think I called you about my zone six?"

"Your rear man-door?" He looked stunned with my confession, but smiled up at me, was completely insatiable for my skin. Kirk Rowdy delivered, "Show me how bad you want it then, Needly."

That was what I wanted as Rowdy became a prerequisite for my evening. I found a fresh condom in a study drawer and tossed it to him. He applied his steeping, nine inch rod with the plastic, and coaxed me over to him. I fixed one leg over his seated and still body, then the other. Immediately, I felt his rod against the opening in my backside, which stirred more desire within me. Mechanically he nibbled at my pecs and nipples, licked my skin, devoured my new sweat, drew his pointed sliver of tongue over my flesh with ease, and left both of us fully committed to each other, content. His palms were locked on my hips as fingers dug gently into my flesh. My body dropped over his massive extension as I planted appendages on his shoulders, arching my neck. Endlessly, I fell onto his manly branch. Helplessly, he left me feel bemused and reckless as inch after inch of his pistol entered me, as his cockhead pivoted my skin open, inflowing with ease as it pushed up and inside me, deeper and deeper, and caused me to groan and gag like a pup, like I had never carried out that act before between two sticky men in a compromised position.

"Deeper," he moaned beneath me, licked my nipples, pulled off, pushed all nine inches into my insides. "Fall on it, Needly. This is why you called me here. Take it all."

I listened to him, happily obliged, fell onto his bulk, rose again, and fell. I had my feet up on the edge of the comfortable couch and rode him with my sweaty palms still connected to his shoulders. And as my eyes fell into the back of my skull, his cock resolutely bolting wildly and hypnotically inside my rear man-door, up and down, in and out, continuously, rapturously, our breaths grew and blended together, both of us escalated within the study. With man connected to man, we rode and pumped, kissed and groaned—man finally and wholly inside man.

As he drove into me, the officer worshiped my skin and body, toyed with my chute, and built a cumbersome load. I felt one of his hands as it released itself from my left hip. He was committed to seeing me come and told me so, explained rather pleasingly, "I want you to shoot on me, Paul … Can you do that?"

I was unable to answer him as he worked my rod up and down. His one hand pushed and pulled on the seven inches of jumping and stirring man-bar. I huffed and puffed overtop him, felt fingers smoothly tantalize veins and skin as our bodies worked together as one, a mechanical man-investigation between us. He stroked my rod with ease as my tight hole buckled around his digested pole. Serenely, we quivered together, groaned naturally and fanatically, and conventionally we burst our loads in a simultaneous manner. Rowdy filled the condom full of his sap as a pop of goo blew from my rod. My spray arced towards his chest and the dimple in his chin, flew out of my spigot with conditional speed. And mutually we became numb and spent, murmured a harmonious opera of man-sex, desire, and lust, as we shot thick loads with ease.

Afterwards, I leaned into him, lapped up my bittersweet load from his chest, kissed him, and lapped up

13

more, I asked with a smile, "You knew it was me who called your radio, didn't you, Rowdy?"

He kissed me hard, pulled off, touched his nose to mine, smiled broadly at me, and responded, "I was hoping it was you, Needly. A guy needs checked out once and a while, doesn't he?"

I answered him by pressing my lips to his, blocked his words, kissed him hard and harder, and attempted something between us, again and again.

RIDE!

~ ~ ~

My arrival at Ranch Briscoe in Texas is … sweaty-sweet. My instructions are simply stated on the back of Dallas Briscoe's business card: *Go to Cabin Longwood, unpack, rest, and meet up with the staff at eight PM in Custard's Hall for introductions.* I'm early, I realize, and after unpacking, decide to meander around the ranch to become acquainted with my new surroundings instead of resting.

Dallas Briscoe's ranch is over three hundred square acres, tucked away in the northwestern part of Texas. There is currently one ranch hand; I'm the newly hired second. The ranch is spacious and arid, a cowboy's dream. Everything is stingingly rich with the scent of hay and barbecue, sweetly tainted with ragweed and Queen Anne's lace.

I easily find my way to the barn, kitchen, and other various interests on the ranch. By a charming and smiling dark-haired Indian boy, I am offered information that the plumbing on the ranch has gone bad, and if I need to bathe, I will have to use the nearby stream. On the southernmost side of the property, I find the tiny stream named Copperhead Creek. I ease up on it slowly, listen to its rushing waters, feel the sullen breeze lick at my bare neck and hands. Crickets chirp crazily in the surrounding fields as I see a Mustang horse tied to the limb of an ancient oak tree. Keeping my view on the horse, I walk directly into a pile of clothes on the hard ground by the stream, stop dead and stare down at the lump: tan colored Stetson hat, jeans with a silver Dustin Stockyard belt, and Ariat Heritage Lacer boots. Immediately, I look up and into the shimmering water and see ... the sexiest, most arrogantly handsome, and naked, cowboy in the creek with soap in hand, bathing. The site of the stranger catches me off guard, causes a flurry of embarrassment to skitter up my neck and redden my pale, boyish cheeks. I stand behind a nearby oak and keep a steady gander on the prime, grade-A beef in Copperhead Creek.

Everything about the thirty year old cowboy is chiseled and hot. As he sits in the clear stream, rolling an orange bar of soap over his dark-golden skin, I see his hazel eyes reflect brilliantly in the evening's light. The Texan's muscles are lined with hard veins that cover his pumped limbs like the lines on a map. He has blonde, wet hair grazing his ab and pec-covered chest. As I lick my lips and feel something madly stir within my Wrangler's, my eyes gawk at the two perfectly hard nipples that are covered with white suds on the steer-man's bulky chest. Slowly, the cowboy rinses in the clear water, stands up, spreads his legs, and then begins to lather up his firm thighs.

With my heart triggering and bouncing in my lean chest, I see the nine inches of dangling, uncut bronco between the cowboy's legs. The Texan moves the bar of creamy soap from one thigh to the next, strong palms working skin and suds and muscles. He then stretches the bar up and over the blonde triangle patch of pubic hairs that looks like canyon brush. Next, the bar of soap slowly moves down the escalating two inch-wide long shaft, in a raw manner. He pulls on the end of his cockhead, stretching the rope-like length with ease and ... possible enjoyment.

He looks like glowing leather in the evening sun. Moistened just right with droplets of oil. Working leather that is smooth and soft ... perfect for my bare hands. The cowboy rinses again, causes his long shaft to grow slightly hard, arched and pointing to the south. He looks up and ... senses someone present ... someone who could be innocent and maybe a new ranch hand. Hottie, rustic *me!*

Our eyes meet in a questionable, connecting manner that usually doesn't take place between assumed straight men. "Who are you?" The cowboy squints his shimmering, grass-green eyes, and asks from the water. He stands with dripping liquid over his iron-crafted body, is completely trim and perfect, already beginning to dry in the quaint, evening breeze.

"Randy ... Randy Marke ... I'm the new ranch hand." I'm nervous and hard, lick my lips with a steady appetite. I can't come out from behind the strong oak because of the limb that's under my denim. With my head cocked to one side of the oak, though, I affix my solid gaze on the man-beef who is interested in determining my interloping.

"Randy the ranch hand," a crisp smile laces the cowboy's face as he begins to walk out of Copperhead Creek, steps up and onto the dry bank with his arched protein swinging in the wind. He introduces himself, "Dallas Briscoe. I believe we talked on the phone ... I offered you the job."

I have to step out from behind the tree to shake his outstretched hand. He notices my long wood under Wrangler's almost immediately, connects magnetic eyes to my denim, smiles faintly, rubs the blonde bristles on the end of his chin with a free hand. As he shakes my nervous palm and fist, still observing and concentrating on my handy goods, Dallas says, "By the looks of you, Randy, ... I think you're going to do just fine on my ranch."

"Thank you." I become more hard. Crazy hard. My hand is strong in his grasp, steady and all power.

Dallas is beyond rock-sharp and studlike. He is a sliver of perfection in front of me, naked with a semi-hard, drooping cock, smiling and candy-handsome ... legendary. He eyes up my bulking chest, Mexican-dark eyes and hair. Eventually, he expires our handshake and places a palm to my tight jaw, turns my head from left to right in a steady and stern manner, checking out my smooth and boylike features. Dallas drops his hand and says, "I know I asked you this on the phone during your interview, but how old are you again?"

"Twenty-four." My eyes shift from his rugged-muscular chest to his long, uncut cock that hangs between wet thighs. It is a stunning thing in the light, and causes my own rod to bounce slightly within my jeans.

He instructs, "Turn around for me, Randy."

I listen to him with ease, because he's my employer, because I don't mind at all, because if I don't he just ...

Dallas presses tight hands into my shoulders, then my biceps, stands directly behind me and continues to instruct, "Lift your arms." He finds the compact muscles on my sides, wraps arms around my crafted and pumped chest, and investigates my lower torso with delicate and probing fingers. "Feels great, dude ... Enough muscle to get the job done around here." Dallas spins my body around then, stares directly down at my crotch, moves his right hand to my package, cups balls and stiffening prod, and nonchalantly asks in his cowboy drawl, "Showing off, aren't you?"

In a cocky manner I respond with a city boy's smile, "Just proving a point that I'm the man for the job."

He likes me, finds me irresistible, perhaps. I have easily fitted his new personalized ranch hand role. Come off as being clever and attractively smooth, which causes Dallas to scrape up a hearty laugh as he massages my rod and hard balls. He catches my eyes with his, whispers in the evening breeze, "Of course you are. Did you get all settled into your cabin?"

I nod my head, respond, "Yes, sir," and stand with my legs parted slightly, with my Adam's apple nervously bobbing up and down.

Dallas slowly rubs his hand against the denim between my legs, hardening up my goods all the way, causing me to feel dizzy and raw. "You going to be a gentleman and take a bath before this evening's introduction to the rest of the staff?"

"Sure." I smile, sound too easy, too naïve and boylike. As I begin to unbutton buckle, buttons, and plaid shirt, I wonder which staff he is going to introduce me to … the group of employees back at the ranch that I will be working with for the next few months, or the piece of man-meat hardening up between Dallas's thoroughbred thighs.

He catches me off guard, steps back a pace, spreads his legs wide and wider. With bronze hands, Dallas grasps his now ten inches of stiffening and rising bull, and begins to tame the beef. He watches me slip out of T-shirt and boots, then jeans. Within seconds, the only thing I'm wearing is a rawhide friendship bracelet that was given to me by a dude in Austin. My juicy, eight inches of donkey protrudes from my lean body. Without any hand-convincing, a smear of ranch goo collects at the tippy-slit of my Dallas-interest.

Briscoe licks his lips, pumps veined and throbbing cock with busy hands, causing the uncut head to pop out of skin. The cowboy keeps his eyes constricted on mine as he informs rather easily, "I think I'll break you in right now, Randy."

"Break me in?" I ask, challenged by his comment. If he plans on using the mighty ten-incher on my hardly used ass … then he'd better have some heavy duty lube, I think.

"Come here, man … Loosen up … I'm not going to hurt you. Everyone needs a little welcome." He's hot and gentle and all blonde-perfection. Dallas trains me easily, moves forward and asks rather politely, with Texas manners, "You have a boyfriend?"

"Not currently," I respond, feel his cock press up against mine, both heads touching, ball-sacks carrying out an invested tango in the heated, now sticky, evening.

"Things really do come big in Texas, don't they?" I ask, eyeing up the massive size of his hardening pounder.

"Yes, siree." The horse tamer gentle collides his chest with mine. Our erect nipples kiss as his tongue meets the elongated and tight shape of my neck. I feel the blonde bristles of his chin-scruff against my flesh. Dallas holds my hips in his large but steady hands, pulls his tongue off of my skin and whispers gallantly into my right ear, "Can a cowboy like me overcome the sight of a handsome, young stranger?"

It's like he's singing one of those sad country songs, or reciting windy poetry. I fall for it, though, chant wisely, "It depends what's in it for me."

His left hand ropes around my field post and his fingers find the smear of guy-ooze. Briscoe pulls the appendages away, finds my lips with my own juice, and whispers, "A little chow, a hot cowboy … and a great big piece of Texas."

I taste his offered chow, swallow the salty-sweet goodness, lick my lips, kiss his rough fingertips, and feel his free hand draw one of my palms to his pulsating rifle. The cowboy kisses me hard, pushing his tongue to the back of my throat as he gently bucks his Randy-poker into my hand with ease.

I'm dizzy and confused against him. Dallas is too steamy and massive to begin an escape from. If I do attempt this, I will merely drop to the arid ground, and become totally abandoned for scavengers. I cling to Dallas's every muscle, working his dick with my right hand, kissing him hard and harder … unbroken.

He smells rustic and masculine, like strong mesquite beside me as I tug up and down on his wild pony. Dallas moans greedily, bites my neck, my right nipple. As he falls to his knees, he finds every tight ab on my lower torso, lapping at each with his extended tongue. With experienced fingers, Dallas grazes the line of midnight colored hair from my naval to the triangle patch of pubes. Slowly, with his cowboy tongue, he moves the head of my cock in and out of his mouth, a stampeding motion that drives me wild, eventually positioning it hard and steady against the smoothness of his throat. He holds onto my hips with both hands, balancing himself, roping me in his arms. And with skill Dallas begins to work his tongue around my muscled rod again, slurping and moaning, totally into me ... the idyllic cowboy at work.

I tour his mouth, humping and thrusting forward, bucking his handsome face wildly. Dallas gently squeezes my nipples, still on his knees. Because I haven't been with a guy in four months, I can't help myself from popping off an immediate and spontaneous load of Randy-glue into my employer's craving mouth. I feel jitters of rhythmic vibrations flood over my entire body, hold onto the back of Dallas's head with both hands, howling at the top of my lungs like a desert wolf.

Beneath me, Dallas gags on his prompt find, swallows some of the guy-stuff, has it rolling out and down the edges of his perfect mouth. The ranch hand goo continues to drip down the length of his lined neck. He releases for air, sucks harder, practically causes me to come twice inside his mouth. His tongue works unwaveringly, lapping up white necessity with ease, taking my cock down his throat, pressing his nose into my dark pubes, groaning like a real Texas cowboy.

Eventually Dallas stands, spreads his legs wide again, has his stallion pointing at my sloped, rippled chest. As his muscled fists rotate up and down on his flesh-horse, Briscoe grits his teeth and then lets out a masculine sound that a coyote might make. Every part of his body is ripped and hard, glistening with new, evening sweat. And because I roll fingers up and down over his chest, helplessly giving in to the supine muscles on his neck with my tongue and lips, pinching nipples, grazing abs with fingertips, he sprays an endless amount of Dallas-juice over my chest, hips, and still-hard cock.

Afterwards, we head into Copperhead Creek together, ready to wash up. Dallas says, "Welcome to Briscoe Ranch, dude ... I think I'm going to like having you around here."

I can't object; Dallas Briscoe is more than all sweaty-sweet man ... he's passed the test to be my new boyfriend.

It's two days later and I'm tucked into the third floor loft of the barn, feeding the horses by forking hay down into clean stalls. Sturdy rafters hang around stacks of golden hay in the sticky and sugary smelling loft. I'm shirtless and hot, ready to take an interim. The afternoon suns shimmies its way through the opened cracks of the barn. I'm breathing hard, completely sweaty and exhausted, have become the perfect skilled ranch hand. I decide to take a short break and lean in through a loft doorway, look out at the expansive view of Briscoe Ranch.

The dry, vast fields go on forever. I see Dallas, taming a stallion in smallish corral, straddling and riding the bucking and wild animal with all his might, hanging on for dear life. Dallas Briscoe's lean and muscular body bounces up and down wildly. Eventually he gets bucked off the pissed stallion. Dallas's tan Stetson goes first, flies down to the dry earth, and then Dallas himself goes careening in mid-air, legs wide open, arms flailing, and lands on his ass. He stands up, brushes himself off with spread legs and bent knees, arched back, in a masculine manner that drives a shiver of excitement up and down my spine. Growing hard and harder in my jeans, I watch him collect his hat and act as if nothing has happened with his cowboy routine.

In the distance, Dallas decides to take a break of his own, slips his shirt and hat off, places both on a fence post. He pours water over his head next. Chilling liquid that decorates his pointed nipples, rounded abs on firm stomach. The water dribbles down over his silver belt buckle of a man riding a steer. It washes Dallas's blonde and stinging chest, cooling him down.

I'm lost within my loft, can't help from pushing down a newly aroused erection. Everything about the moment is heated and erotic ... just watching Dallas perform his everyday procedures. Fortunately, I'm alone and decide rather easily to undo buckle and belt, allow Wrangler's to fall down to my ankles. As my view rests on Dallas from below with his created soothing waterfall, I latch sweaty palms onto extended and firm cock, start working the nine inches of fork with ease, spread my legs as far as they will go, buck hips and ass forward, turning myself on. Everything about my body is sweaty and stinging. Closing my eyes, I catch breaths of hay-filled air, groan mildly, work a stallion of my own, am ready to pop a load of creamy me right now, ready to ...

Loose boards squeak behind me. "Why don't you use that thing on me, Randy?" Immediately, I spin around and see Dallas in the loft with me. He is wearing his hat, but is shirtless and sweaty, drop dead gorgeous and rippled. He has his arms stretched above his head, is practically hanging from a rafter. I see the blonde curls under his pits, the pumped lines on his terrain-like chest. His jeans are unbuckled and I view his drooping piece of cowboy dream between his legs.

I'm holding onto Randy rawhide with both hands, feel a tiny spurt of pre-jism at the top of my protruding Dallas-finder. "You scared the shit out of me."

"Didn't mean to ... I just came to see if you could break me." His veined shaft is growing by the second, becoming hard and harder, rising to the occasion of two hot and sexy men in a sun-bleached loft.

"Break you?" I ask.

The equestrian god nods his head, reaches down between his legs with his pumped, right hand, shares a delicious smile with me, and responds, "It's time for you to be handy, Randy."

Some of the rafters are low in the loft and Dallas hangs from one with his legs and ass spread wide open. Wearing nothing but his tan Stetson, Dallas lays on a bale of hay and peers up at me with infiltrating desire in his hazel eyes, begs, "Take a lick of my horse."

I listen to him, draw my tongue up the smooth length of his bronco, position lips over sultry, rigid cock, and begin to suck him off like the good ranch hand that I am. My tongue ropes the head of his splinter, plays wildly with the excess cock-skin, working it up and down, driving Dallas into a mad frenzy as he cries out like a delirious wildcat. I pinch his nipples and run fingers down over each of his abs, suck his Texas dong with pride and skill, with an almighty tongue that is quite ... handy itself. I lasso his meat with ease, cause him to hump and grind my mouth until he is ready to burst his load.

Quickly, I seize my lapping and licking before Briscoe ruptures. Kneeling between his opened legs, the cowboy's clean-shaven ass glows at me. It's the hottest dude's tight slit that I have ever seen, smirking at me for some practicing tongue-action. With my cock burning hard between my legs, I spread Dallas's slit with tongue, probe him with saliva and slippery extension, cause him to hum wildly on the bale of hay, clenching palms onto the lumber above his head.

He's no Texas rose. Dallas is everything rough and tender. He responds to my action, "You're driving me crazy, dude ... Ride it now ... Break my ass like a bronco."

There is a condom in his jeans that I fetch, saddle it onto my nine inches of loft-fun. I position myself between his legs, rub my cock-tip against his needy, tight hole.

Dallas arches his neck back, still hangs onto the rafter, spreads his legs wider, and informs, "Tame it, Randy ... right now!"

Immediately, I push three inches of my nine into Briscoe's ranch, cause him to call out my name. I pull out with ease, and then quickly rush four inches into his opened man-stable, beginning to tame him. With skill I hold onto his ankles, kick his pressurized ass like an angry horse, bucking him smoothly like a jackrabbit, opening up his Dallas-slit with five inches, six inches, and then a heaping, bulbous seven.

Dallas thunders, "You're making me spurt, Randy-man."

I see a line of pre-ooze wash against the cowboy's lower torso. He's so turned on by my bucking and riding that he can't keep his whole load in. The white sap decorates his fine, golden hair on his tight abs and smooth naval. His pulsating rod bounces to my movement, is completely ready to burst with very little touching, grazing, licking, or …

"Time for some chow," I groan above him, loosen my right hand from his ankle, reach for his goo and lap up some with two fingers. The Dallas-liquid tastes sweet, causes my dick to grow more firm, and allows me to stampede Briscoe's field with the last of my two inches. Promptly, I grind, glide, bolt, race, and plow his suctioned Randy-prize. My movements are careful and galvanized, perfectly rhythmical and pounding-hard.

Dallas can't help himself, whines up to me with wide eyes and stretched neck cords, "I'm broken, dude … Completely broken." He latches one of his hands on his steaming, ten inches and begins to rotate a palm and fingers over the uncut rope.

As the sticky-hard cowboy beats his own stallion, I quickly pull out of him, rip off the condom and stand above him with my legs spread wide open and my cock directly pointed over his rising and falling chest. Together we form a rodeo of hands and cocks bouncing up and down, eyes locked on each other's steamy bodies, teeth gritting and jaws locked. We thrust our hips wildly in a synchronized motion, continuous gyrations flooding through our bodies, man connected to man vibrations that are endlessly jolting.

Duo lines of spew fly out of our stately erections. The white fluid washes over Dallas's torso, painting him with an Indian language. We huff and blow in shared and exasperated manners. The sticky man-glue clings to Dallas with ease. His golden, Lone Star body is now glazed with white, cowboy and ranch hand secretions, decorating his abs and pecs, chin and neck, shoulders and nipples.

Breathing heavily, completely spent in the loft of the barn, I lean forward, slip under the rafter with Dallas, and stick my chest to his, sealing us together, locking our cock-stems into a stinging kiss. I place lips over Dallas Briscoe's mouth, enjoy a long kiss with him, pull off, and ask, "Do I win a blue ribbon prize?"

Dallas surprises me next, rolls me over on the bale of hay, escapes out from under the rafter, and melts me by pushing my legs apart, beginning something new between us, explaining, "As soon I'm done saddling you up for *my* ride, boyfriend."

ON THE FORCE

~ ~ ~

"Toy, are you positioned for action?" I listened to Blake Stevenson ask from behind me, rubbing his crotch into my backside, breathing heavily into my ear … perhaps teasing me.

"Clear," I chanted steadily back, hypnotized by the moonlit night as blood gushed to every bulging muscle in my soldierlike body, and breathed in his warm sweat and musky cologne.

We were on South Way, anticipating excitement. I was harboring a semi-erection in navy work slacks, overwhelmed with masculine adrenaline as Stevenson pressed his nine-inch goods into me, rubbing his covered-cock against my ass and the back of my thighs. It was my first sting with dreamy-eyed Stevenson and his chiseled good looks. The plan was simple: a drug deal was going on in the warehouse by one of the city's most sleaziest; Stevenson and I were posted on South Way; there was an undercover cop doing the dealing inside; and we had six other hotties (nicknamed The Bang Gang) who were ready to bust in a side door and nab Mr. Naughty.

"Is your pistol cocked?" Stevenson asked as he slowly reached around me and cupped my growing man-pouch, fingered the prize with heavy interest and delectable needs.

"I'm good, dude … How about getting serious now?"

He whispered behind me, "I've been through this a thousand times, Marcus. The showdown's about to happen and the bad guy always gets caught … just like I've caught you."

He was toying with me, manipulating my twenty-four year old staff, firming up my rod and balls, needing a high of his own like an addict on the street. Stevenson was into *everything* about me (rosy cheeks, smooth chest, muscles in all the right places, six foot-plus frame), called me the hottest cop on the force, and whispered occasionally to me, "You're mine, Toy … Don't forget that."

I smiled in front of him in silence as a few seconds passed. I imagined Blake Stevenson standing in front of me with his five-eleven stance, almond colored eyes, blonde spiked hair, gumdrop dimples in cheeks, and razor-sharp jaw. Every time my gaze passed over his Olympian-type body at Station 2469, something twirled deviously and temperamentally within my chest, melting me. I liked him— maybe too much.

And there against the warehouse's metal structure I waited with patience as he teased me prior to the sting's breakdown. Our inside man was ready. The Bang Gang was ready. I was sweaty and fired-up and …

Stevenson—with a handy skill—unbuttoned two buttons near my silver shield and gradually slid his right palm between T-shirt and uniform. Teasingly, slowly, and tempestuously he began playing with my right nipple, firming it up and exciting me as he coyly nipped at my neck with a moist kiss, murmuring into my ear, "Did I ever tell you how hot you look in blue, Toy?"

Quite dizzy and uncomfortable, hard as steel between my legs, I pulled my neck away from his kiss and chanted sedately, "Stop it, Blake … save it for another day."

He giggled. And I couldn't help but to giggle back.

Then shockingly there were two quick gunshots inside the warehouse. Some lug was screaming atrocious profanities. The preconceived plan was breaking down, turning into a bust. Everything was going wrong. I stood shaking, ready with my Colt cocked, still hard between my legs, trembling and feeling wild, licked my lips, and waited.

Stevenson immediately pulled his hand away from my pumped chest and positioned himself like a hero next to me on South Way—ready for the unexpected.

Seconds passed before a mouth in the warehouse's wall tore open about four feet to the left of us. A black Caddy with tinted windows buzzed out. And once it was on South Way some druggie lord popped his arm out a passenger's window and shot three times.

One bullet hit the aluminum wall above Stevenson's head. Another shell whizzed off to our right. The third slug struck me in the chest, knocking me to the ground—instantly.

As I laid on the pavement, observing a million twinkling-disco-shining stars in the night, I listened to Stevenson's panicked and wavering voice as he screamed into his walkie-talkie, "Man down! … Man down! … Toy's down!"

What's a dude to do when forced to take a few days off from work because of a shot to the left shoulder? I read a little, watched a lot of porn, and talked on the phone. Visitors came by my apartment with gifts, cards, and … *kisses?*

Stevenson popped in with Chevy Reese, another police officer from our team. Reese brought pizza coupons stuffed in a get well card and Stevenson came empty-handed. We talked for about an hour: duty gossip and masculine sports. Each of us had a Rolling Rock. The guys left, both telling me to get better, rest up, and that the force missed and needed me.

Once alone, to my right, on the end table where I kept the TV's remote control, I saw Stevenson's Dolce & Gabbana sunglasses. I was just getting ready to call his cell when three taps on the door followed: "Toy, I left my shades on your table!"

"Door's open!" I blared from where I sat on the over-stuffed couch, smiling.

Stevenson opened the door, slid up to the table, ever-so-slightly leaned into me and brushed a hand against my inner-thigh, shared a smile with me that was drop-dead cute and somewhat intoxicated like the Rolling Rock, leaving me say rather light-headedly, "Let me guess, you left them there on purpose, didn't you?"

He laughed, "How'd you know?" with his face only inches from mine.

"You haven't rubbed up against me in two full days ... Something was telling me you were needy. A guy like you can't live without me."

Stevenson leaned into me more then, connected his perfectly almond orbs with my walnut ones, kissed me hard, slipped his tongue down the back of my throat, locked his lips against my own, and rolled his right hand against my inner-thigh, causing a blend of fiery turbulence to bolt through my cock and balls, melting me. After that mind-faltering kiss, I rubbed a hand across my shivering mouth and breathed, "I'm not your boyfriend, Stevenson."

He moved away from the couch leaving me hard and horny, chanting over his shoulder, "I never said you were my boyfriend, Toy. Just take that as your get well gift ... and your medicine." Stevenson vanished then with his shades; I stayed hard wondering when he would return again.

I craved his closeness, desiring him. Badge number 7814 was hot, sexy, and down-right perfect for me—the man of my dreams, a healthy dose of life and hardening perseverance. I wasn't surprised when he arrived two days later with a dashing and darling smile smeared over his blonde face. And nor was I shocked when Stevenson swept me to his cottage in Big Sur.

It was beautiful there: tall trees, comfy breeze, and a pleasantly mediocre temperature. Stevenson had me out on this stretch of opened lawn that was encased by redwoods—his own personal shooting range. He had a number of bull's eye targets set up at different distances and wanted me to practice shots with him. There was no one out there—just the two of us, men behaving like men, the air clean and just perfect. It was like a date or something with Stevenson, without the bar scene or the Oakland A's or Raiders—it was like he purposely *caught me* up there at Big Sur, pleading his case of likeness for me and sharing some healing time.

"You're too wobbly, dude," he laughed from behind me. I was trying to fire off a Colt .45 using one hand. As one arm rested against my chest in a sling, fresh bandages on my healing shoulder, my other arm and hand awkwardly swirled in a dangerous circle. I couldn't hit the one-hundred foot target if my life depended on it.

"I'm having problems, Blake. This isn't easy."

"Do you need some help?"

"No … let me try."

He didn't give me the opportunity to try on my own. Stevenson immediately crept up behind me, wrapped a gentle arm around my middle, breathed amiably on the nape of my neck, raising my dark hairs, clamped his right palm over mine, lifted his left hand and found the left side of the pistol, and leaned into me with his pelvis as it pressed nicely against my behind, and coached, "I've got you covered, Toy. Stevenson's here for you."

"Because you're my partner," I whispered.

"You got it … now aim and shoot."

I couldn't fire the Colt. I was shivering from his breath against my neck and the soft hairs on his chin as they caressed my skin. I swallowed saliva in my mouth with nervousness, stunned by his attraction and closeness for me, completely overwhelmed by his sensitive lure to me. Sweetly

31

and softly I chattered, "You're toying with me, aren't you, Blake?"

"Don't you want me to?"

It was unbelievable—I liked him too much. I had this throttling crush on him that was immeasurable. Throughout the first months while working with him I had created a sexual mind-affair. And what was best about it all, Stevenson liked me ... and we were secluded, lost in Big Sure—just the two of us. I chanted rather whimsically, "What do you want, Stevenson ... a partner against crime or ..."

The pistol fired twice because I was trembling and unsteady, because I was lost in the moment, captivated by him ... because we were together in silence, his cock rubbing against my back side, his breath on my neck, his closeness like a street drug.

In a heroic and vigorous manner he spun me around by my waist and peeled the Colt from my hand, complimented me casually, "Congratulations, you made a bull's eye, Toy."

"But I wasn't even close to the target," I responded.

Charming Stevenson replied, "Trust me ... you hit it right on," and blocked my argument with moist lips as he locked his left hand against my back and gently moved my shivering body towards him, sealing us together.

It was a kiss that was serious and potent, like a rush after catching a bad guy. Stevenson pushed his tongue into the tunnel of my throat, pulled his hand away from my back and touched my T-shirt covered abs beneath the sling. The kiss was emphatic and breathtaking, mind-numbing and relaxing—as if it were meant to be. And after seconds in his tongue and mouth world, spellbound by his gentle captivity, he pulled away, and rushed his speech, "You're too good for me, Toy, do you know that?"

I didn't have time to answer him. Stevenson peeled off his black tee and tossed it to the ground, clicked the Colt's chamber open and set it down on the shirt. I was far too mesmerized by his bristly, blond hairs lining the center of his chest, falling and falling into his tight jeans. It was one of those perfect chests you see in *Men's Fitness* or *Gym*—something desirable and ripped with perfection, absolutely cock-hardening. My eyes didn't stop there, though, and continued to gaze with a southward fixation. Pupils locked on nine inches of outlined cock in his jeans, which caused me to embarrassingly lick my lips.

Stevenson ran a hand over his spiked hair (bicep on arm bulged as tiny spot of hair under his pit became quite visible) and playfully asked, "What are you looking at, Marcus Toy?"

I didn't know how to respond. Had I fallen for him? Was I toying with myself about man falling into man, needing his comfort and closeness, simply allowing my mind-set to tumble into the depths of his hearty and healthy looking body? And what was with the goods firming up between my legs: eight full inches of cut cock ready to burst a load in my own jeans.

"Toy?" he laughed.

"You're … you're …" I began stuttering.

"Hard for you," he completed the rest of my sentence. "Absolutely hard and crazy for you, Toy … Now what do you say we appease these emotions and act like real partners?"

There was a circle of stumps next to the edge of the woods where he told me to lean into a redwood as he unbuttoned my jeans. Stevenson laughed, "You're not wearing anything underneath, Toy."

"Underwear are too hard to put on … I just skip that process."

He cupped my sack in one hand as he released my stiff eight inches of pole. Slowly and meticulously Stevenson began to lick the poker with his pointed tongue, staring up and over the sling and my T-shirt, eating me whole. Inch after wholesome inch swelled in his throat as he gagged and choked, practically caused him to become half-suffocated beneath me. And dizzily I searched for balance. My world spun in warmly mad circles as I felt keenly capable of popping off a creamy loud into his mouth. Eventually I had to tell him, "Stop, Blake ... I'm going to fall and then my arm will never get better."

With comfort and care he pulled off my package, licked his lips, rubbed the back of his right hand across his mouth and suggested I sit down on one of the stumps. I listened and kept my legs spread open for him after he yanked my jeans down and off. The stump was rough on my asscheeks as his tongue was friendly with my weapon again. Beneath me he enjoyed the inches, sucking and inhaling on the loaded tool, groaning and slurping. Stevenson was captivated and awestruck by the meat as he played with my balls, caressing them with available fingers, occupying himself with his woodsy find—*me!*

Fully thrusting my mass into his mouth, quite capable of raising my weight up and off the stump with one hand, I allowed my furry balls to smack against his face. Quickly I bolted my rod into his throat, deeper and deeper, choking him, watching his back like a good partner, keeping him covered with my moving shadow in the afternoon sun. I bucked wildly, filled him whole, and pulverized his mouthy suction with eight inches of ripped cock. And above him, admiring his back muscles in motion, his lats and V-shaped niceness, I whimpered, "It's a sting, Blake ... and this is a showdown."

He pulled off and responded, "I'm positioned and ready."

I pushed his head towards my body and explained, "You'd better be, Stevenson ... because this is what you've been craving."

As Stevenson enjoyed the taste of my skin, melting beneath me, I continued to ram and plow the sliver of his mouth, blow after blow. Time created our digestible romp, leaving me filled with eager delight, half-occupied with an impulsive action of spewing a load into him, ejaculating the creamy satisfaction too soon. When that shivering and emphatic feeling washed over me, I pushed Blake away and groaned wildly, "Not here … Not yet. I want you to make it last … Tease me more."

The cottage's atrium was a glass-walled structure surrounded by the Big Sur woods. There was a comfy settee the color of springtime ferns which Stevenson laid down on after stripping out of his clothes. I gawked hungrily at his solid pecs, the line of hair dragging between his firm abs, blonde curls that made up a pubic triangle above his nine inches of uncut firearm in durable plastic.

Naked myself, arm still in sling, I whispered to him, "Is that thing loaded and cocked?"

Stevenson looked up at me in a dazed, contented, and blissful manner. He chanted playfully, "Come here and try it out, dude."

How ravenous I was for Blake Stevenson. How pained it seemed to pass up on one of the most nicely structured, awestruck blondes, and precisely perfect bodies at Station 2469. And how determined I was not to pass up on the opportunity. Thirsty for his body against mine I moved towards him and stepped carefully over his flattened body with his legs bent and feet locked onto the wooden floor.

"Do you have a license for that thing?" he asked, playing with the helmet on my revolver, teasing it with two fingers, causing pre-come to leak out the tip of its cut throbber.

"You bet your ass?"

He laughed, "How about your ass, Toy?" and consumed the spew from his fingers, drawing them against his slightly opened lips.

"Whatever it takes, guy … I'm yours."

After his afternoon taste of Toy-food, Stevenson delicately held onto my hips and began to slip his rod into me. Once positioned on top of him, Blake clasped his right hand onto my cock and began moving its excess skin up and down, calling up to me, "You're one of the bad guys, aren't you, Toy?"

I wanted to respond to his question, but couldn't. After two inches entered my tight sliver, silky-dark balls meeting his torso, and shaft standing at full attention, I began gritting my teeth. Unhurriedly and gradually three inches entered my guy-hole, then a forth ... fifth ... sixth. With new pain gliding throughout my world—a rookie spinning prosaically above his trainer—I tightly closed my eyes and took the last three inches in. Consumed. Detained. Captured. Finally Stevenson's.

My innocence was lost. I was riding him wildly, passionately, and resolutely. Again and again I rose and fell over his nine inches of column and allowed it to slip deeper into me, pushing up between my ribs, frisking me. His beef toyed with my insides, friction burning my ass ... pushing and pushing. It was harmonious and endless, fervent and tender, cop inside cop, partners working together, grinding bodies in a fiery union—everlasting.

And there I was ... on the force, creating an erotic and masculine rhythm with his Colt-like cock, positioned above him, straddling his perfectly sculpted body as I teased his blonde chest hairs with straying fingers, moaning and groaning atop his flesh. Slowly, wickedly, contemptibly, I careened against him, the glass-atrium echoing with our swelling voices, his Redwood thumping my insides, bolting upwards and into me, spreading me apart with ease and a steady grinding that was structurally persuasive. Our motion was real and breathtaking—an urgency between two men. As he bucked my hole I revolved around his device with a sweltering and mind-blowing agenda of my own. It was an action that was needed and confined between men, sexual sameness that was blissful and idyllic ... ours.

Stevenson worked my rod with speed: steadily, engrossingly, and vigorously. His hand-movement caused me to call out, "Stevenson, it's time for a breakdown."

"The sting, Toy ... Go for it," he murmured between my legs, glowing and smiling, numb with my ass-movements.

Quickly I pulled off him and stepped to his right side, watched him toss the condom to the atrium's floor. As Stevenson began to strum his own tool—hand over hand, working fiercely and promisingly—I stepped back slowly ... one foot ... two feet ... the experienced shooter at work, a handy firearm between my strong thighs, and positioned myself in front of Blake, warning him, "You'd better take cover for your own safety."

Stevenson groaned madly as his fist pumped veined rod, "Ready when you are."

I was not overtop of his fixation but could still feel his nine inches inside me. With my right hand I rocked my meat up and down a few times, knowing it wouldn't take long to shoot. I thrust hips forwards, backwards, forwards again and again, simply arched my back, breathed heavily as fingers stayed busy, called out his name three times, and sprayed my load—drop after silky white drop—onto Blake's golden skin. Warmly I coated the area between his chest and compact legs, fired shot after shot of goo against his skin. And while doing so—stinging him with my goods—I was left bemused because of my own actions, and charmingly called out, "Man down! ... Man down, Stevenson!"

"You're mine, Toy ... all mine," he called up to me.

Completely red-faced and dizzy, bolting hips to and fro, feeling nostalgic and unreal, harder than hard, I sweetly and tantalizingly rolled fingers up and down on my gun, positioning it over him, wildly spraying him with my liquid bullets, draining the tool, quickly becoming unsteady, losing my balance, and spent.

And beneath me, wide-eyed and sweaty, gritting his teeth, I knew that Stevenson was burning with an emphatic gesture to shoot his own load towards me. Hand over hand he worked his tool, aiming it towards me. Stevenson murmured in an untamable manner as he continuously thrust his hips upwards, closed his eyes, and spat, "Look out, Toy … I'm firing."

And like the night on South Way in the city at the warehouse I became remarkably stunned as one come-bullet fired over my head. The second goo-shell whizzed off to my right. But it was the third spew-slug that struck me in the chest, exactly where the bullet had hit me—instantly.

Crazily I moved towards him, found the third shot on the sling with three fingers, and recited dramatically, "You shot me, Stevenson."

He laughed on the settee, finishing his work, flinging extra goo-droplets from his spike to the solid blonde plain of chest, mixing our come together, "Some friendly fire."

I sat down with my legs straddled over the green settee. Stevenson sat up. And with our sticky legs entwined, eyes connected, Blake kissed me hard, wrapping fingers around my still-hot gun, playing with me. I held him against me carefully and closely, inhaled his thick sweat and musky fragrance. Slowly I pulled away with ease, and boyishly whispered, "The bad guy always gets caught, doesn't he, Blake?"

His almond eyes twinkled as his chest heaved in and out. Stevenson cuddled his pecs against my healing arm and breathed softly, "Always, Toy … Always," and sealed us together with another kiss.

SNOWBLOWN

~ ~ ~

Mount Apalli, Colorado. Height: 1,269 feet. Population: two. Weather conditions: mostly sunny and thirty-one degrees Fahrenheit. Chance of precipitation: thirty percent. Odds of two hot and hard guys getting it on while becoming stranded: pretty good.

Mount Apalli is chiseled like a weightlifter's pumped back and tight ass. It's icy and rocky looking, perfectly jutting with a maximum degree of winter niceness. The mountain is bitchin' and rude, totally rough and dick-jolting. Puffy white powder decorates the razor-sharp rocks and massive trees as I stand at its base, take the winter-fresh moment into my lungs, and feel a splinter of wood perk up in my Columbian suit. Everything about the moment is real and exhilarating, a total turn on for me.

"Dude, you coming?" It's Dex Remington, Apalli's most skilled field ranger. He's all bright and happy, blond and blue-eyed, beyond a pup, and unquestionably rock-hard handsome. Dex is simply adorable with his dimples and broad shoulders, his everlasting glow of twenty-seven year old goodness, a champion lifesaver during the most severe winter predicaments, a mountain climber, rescuer, and ... snow god.

"I'm coming. Just taking the moment in."

Dex is totally into me, can't stop gawking at me. He absorbs my chocolate eyes and boyish good looks, consumes my V-shape of prime muscles and sculpted jaw, perhaps finds me richly attractive, available, and stingingly hot. He smiles at my comment as a twinkle shines between narrow lips on a white cuspid in the afternoon sun. "If you take too long, McCallen, all the snow's going to melt."

Side by side we hike to the top of Apalli, man with man, share the same water bottle, and talk about the new position I'm interviewing for as his assistant field ranger. Dex wants to see what kind of man I'm made of, defines his interviewing technique as being "rigorously challenging in the outdoors." He doesn't believe in a lot of paperwork or test scores, informs me rather methodically, "Cade, it's about muscle and man ... the wild frontier and the means of survival. If you get through today with me, you've got the job."

So far, today is a piece of cake. I dove into thirty-one degree water, climbed a blue pine the size of a skyscraper, and bolted through a cyclone of fire and saved a human-shaped dummy, passing all three challenges with flying colors. Hip-hip hooray!!!

Now, Dex is putting me through another physical test, ski slope survival. After slipping into Tundra X2 skis, the snow dude informs me at the top of Apalli, "I'm heading down. If you pass this test ... I'll see you at the bottom." He holds out an impressive hand for me to shake, says, "Good luck, man ... Apalli has a body count and I hope you're not an addition to its total." Dex Remington swishes down the hill like some mountain ghost; he's by my side one minute, and gone the next.

I'm at the tippy-top of Apalli watching Dex's tiny body zigzag down the slope. My mind lingers and I start thinking: *he's the hottest and most handsome guy in Colorado, rugged and charming, granite-solid and—*

Jesus, he tumbles, begins to roll down Apalli like a snowball. Skies go flying with poles. The ranger cartwheels down the slope in spinning circles like a rag doll. He stops instantly and lands on his back, next to a hulking pine. Dex isn't moving. Dex is in trouble.

Rescue mode kicks in. After slipping goggles over eyes, I immediately push off the top of Apalli with three years of skiing experience under my belt. I dash to the left and then the right, steer around sharp boulders and nasty pines. Snow shifts and flies up behind my working ass. I rush down to Dex's side, nervous as hell, thinking he's dead, and that Apalli has a higher body count. I drop poles and kick off skis, toss goggles and gloves into the snow, and fall to Dex's unmoving body.

After brushing snow away from his face, gently pushing back closed eyelids, I see that his pupils are dilated. Slowly, I lean into his smooth looking lips, practically brush them with my own, and find that he's breathing. Dex Remington is still alive, thank God. I'm about to pull away when he swiftly raises an arm and hand around me, traps me to his hulking, material-covered chest. As I fall haphazardly over and on top of him, our mouths become millimeters apart as hips rest together. Dex begins to breathe regularly, smiles beneath me, and says, "Not bad timing, Cade … If this were a real emergency, I'd think you could save me."

Our eyes blend together, mountainous brown with perilous blue. He smiles beneath me, holds me against him. "I thought you were dead, Dex. And all along you were fucking with me."

He gently shakes his dashing head. "I was not fucking with you, McCallen, I was testing you."

"Did I pass?" I'm hypnotized by his eyes, see us: *showering together in a hot spray; cuddling naked before a skin-warming fire; nestled in his hulking arms as he plunges his ten escalating inches of—*

"Don't know yet, Cade."

"What do you mean you don't know yet?" I begin to push off him, but can't. He keeps me compressed to his body, man-bliss gluing us together.

"There's another quick test."

"What kind?"

"CPR, McCallen. Doesn't a snow-banked guy like me look like he's a little bit needy for some air?"

I smile down at him as he raises his head and kisses me. Our mouths lock together as eight inches of rock-fun immediately spurts to life in my snow pants. I'm dizzy and complacent, feel a liquidy-warmness form in my boxers underneath my winter suit. The moment is awkward, though, and I find myself pulling off Dex Remington. I feel lost and confused, and shy away from his needy mouth and lips.

"What's wrong, McCallen?"

"I've never kissed a guy before."

He smiles at me, pulls his gloves off, caresses one of my cheeks with a free hand, brushes fingers across my mouth, and asks, "How old are you again?"

"Twenty-one."

"The cutest dude like you at twenty-one and you've never been kissed by a guy yet. Maybe I can show you some tricks of the trade," he quips. "This could be a winter wonderland for both of us, huh?"

"Maybe." I swallow saliva in my mouth with wide eyes and feels nervous all over.

I learn that Dex Remington is a gentleman and he doesn't attempt another kiss with me. He helps me up and we begin our cross-country ski along the base of Mount Apalli back to his log cabin in the secluded woods. While briskly shuffling through the snow, Dex asks, "What brings a young guy like you to a mountain like this, anyway?"

"I like the rough and wild kind of life."

"You've got plenty of that around here, McCallen … You stick with me and—"

He looks up and gazes at the rocky and snowy folds of Mount Apalli. There's an instance of silence and then a thunderous *whooooshing* noise. Everything begins to shake around us, rocking and rolling. The white-capped mountain is beginning to fall, spilling snow down its steep slope.

Dex immediately rushes to my side in his skis, cups his massive arms around me in a firm huddle, as if we are hugging, kissing, enveloping. The last thing I feel is a thick embrace of warmness against my neck and then lips as Dex kisses me. And the last thing I hear from him before we are covered in four feet of snow is: "It's an avalanche, McCallen … I'll save you."

We are underneath the avalanche's fury for one day, two days … I'm not sure. I sleep for what feels like forever and dream of wrestling in the snow with Dex, naked bodies twisting together, tongues touching, ball-sacks swinging concurrently, thighs perspiring, arms entangled with legs, and torsos clinging against each other. It's the most erotic dream I've ever had: stinging, hardening, and playful.

I eventually wake and dig for what seems to be hours to freedom and safety through the thickly packed snow. I find Dex in the same hole I've dug. This is no test, I realize. This is reality, debris of an avalanche; post-trauma. To my surprise, I find skis but no poles, carry Dex over my shoulders, and find his cabin two miles away where I will attempt to nurture him back to health.

As it snows for hours on end, I sit beside his bed and whisper, "It was an avalanche, Dex … I'll save you." This time he stirs awake and I try to coax him out of his semi-coma. "Dex?"

His eyeballs flutter beneath eyelids.

"Dex, it's a winter wonderland outside. We've been snowblown."

His eyes slightly open and he sees me, attempts to whisper, "McCa—" and then he's gone, again.

I feed him soup and water for two days, keep him warm by the heat of a licking fire, read and talk to him. He sleeps deeply, maybe dreaming of me, cupping and caressing me, kissing and holding me, saving me—something.

He has a mild scrape on his left cheek from our frozen experience together. Other than this tiny blemish, Dex Remington is flawless. I decide that it is implicit to bathe him. I caress his blond chest with warm soapy water, and eventually rinse it clean. I caress nipples and strong looking abs with an orange sponge, gently lift the soft eight inches of his cock and clean it, then his blond-furry sack that droops between his opened legs. He's the first man I've ever touched … the most beautiful man. Dex is truly a snow god, utterly handsome and perfectly muscled, a relic before my eyes—my incapacitated patient.

After finishing his bath, I can't help it as the sleeping man-need between my thumping legs stirs awake. Six inches grow into seven, and then a pulsating, rippled eight. As his chest rises and falls, Dex breathing, I slip out of my flannel shirt and unzip my jeans. I finger the eight inches of my veined shaft, smear spit on its length, firm it up real hard, begin to work it steadily, in a rhythmic—

I can't do it … not while he's asleep; not while Dex Remington is in that other, white-washed world. I *won't* do it. It's just not right. He's half-comatose, sleeping. Instead, I decide rather conventionally to slip away from his still body and take care of myself in my own bed, visualize our bodies molded together, and shoot a load on my chest, nipples, and even my chin. Satisfied.

It's four days after I rescue Dex from the avalanche. The cabin is hotter than hell and I have the flannel sheets pushed down to my ankles, wearing nothing but boxers. I'm out for about two hours when I wake up to liquid dripping on my bare chest. I open my eyes and become astonished, completely mesmerized, and believe I've been swept away into a homo-dreamworld.

It's not a dream, though. It's for real. It's about muscle and man, survival of the fittest. It's about Dex Remington standing to my right and positioned above me, the fire behind him illuminating his carved silhouette. He's completely naked, buffed and rippled with an extension of ten inch rod sticking directly out of the blondish, triangle of pubic hair. Seeping from the slit-tip of his ten inches are droplets of white syrup onto my right nipple.

"Dex?" I sit up and stare into his intoxicating eyes, feel the sticky ooze clinging to a hardened nipple. "Dex, you're awake?"

He places his right hand onto his stiff shaft and pushes out another drop of cum onto my chest. Dex gazes down at me, is sweaty and delicious looking. "How old are you, Cade?" he whispers as the fire cracks and churns behind him.

I am completely helpless, taken aback, cannot stop looking into his narcotic-blue eyes. With helpless breath trying to escape my lungs, I stutter, "I'm twenty-one."

"And never been touched, right?"

I slightly shake my head. "Never."

The awakened Dex reaches down and collects a glaze of spew onto two fingers and slips them up to my lips, placing the fingers into my parted mouth. "Do you want a rigorous challenge, McCallen?"

His jizm tastes bittersweet on my tongue; it's the first I've ever had guy-juice before and I like it. As Dex feeds me, he gracefully rubs a thumb against my cheek. "You up for another test?"

Before I can breathe in a somewhat normal manner, in and out, steadily, he continues to smile above me. I gaze from his sliver of lips up to his impassive eyes, and then to the swelled cock in the ranger's right hand. Dex slips the fingers out of my mouth, allows me to answer. "I never ... I never—"

He whispers, "You've never done it with a guy before, right?"

I'm nervous as hell, out of my league, and completely trapped under his closeness. I decide rather methodically that there is nowhere to go and that whatever Dex Remington wishes to carry out, I will easily oblige.

"You're shivering."

"I can't help it."

"It's nothing more than jitters because this will be your first time with a guy."

"I don't know what to do," I respond with a wavering voice.

"Just relax. I won't hurt you. I promise." He gradually slips his right hand forward and touches the brown triangle between my legs, weaves fingers into the bristly curls. "It's all about the bodies of men and senses, McCallen." He leans over and into me, licks my stomach with an extended tongue, then breathes my innocence into his flared nostrils.

I slightly jump with a nervous twitch under his tongue. Following the seconds when the ranger rises from my chest, his right palm exits my pubes and rolls up the splay of my steel-like chest. The fingers find abs and nipples with ease. Nimble fingertips pinch the molded nipples, one by one. I go crazy almost immediately as my stiff rod—in the most timely fashion—lifts and falls by itself. A moan or gasp escapes my mouth next as Dex leans over me again, brushing his tongue against my right nipple as chin hair caresses my somewhat perspiring chest.

"I ... I feel lighter."

He responds by lapping at both nipples, finds my overgrown rod in his right hand. I feel Dex's fingers play with the veined cock-skin, mastering it with fingertips and palm, teasing the extension of meat-goodness. The ranger inhales as he laps up my sweat, creating my lower torso to grow hard and harder, challenging me to become experienced, and causing me to feel half-conscious, misplaced with his touching and licking.

"I ... I'm going to faint."

But the moment within the cabin only rises with more virginal satisfaction. As he plays with my throbbing and ready-to-burst pole, I feel his tongue in the back of my throat. It's romantic and kind, sweetness between men, completely likeable. He kisses me for what seems to be forever, whispers tranquilities and endearments into my mouth, becomes a comforting coach. And next—with only moments ticking by in the newly derived snow storm on Mount Apalli—he eventually replaces tongue with the tip of his cock, whispering down to me, "This will tell if you're into guys, McCallen?"

Dex stands over me, slips the meat-piece into my mouth, pulls out, pushes it inside my saliva-cave again. The sweaty tube of pulsating and rippled cock tastes warm and sweet as it presses against the back of my throat. I gag on it once, now twice, but Dex only responds by pivoting more of its hulking ten inches into my mouth. I feel as if I could die it's this large, delicious, and poetically convincing. Beneath him, I slip into a world of unbiased decisions and mediocrity as the chunk of protein staff slides down my throat, gagging me in a rapturous manner. I think: *he's the hottest and most handsome guy in Colorado, rugged and charming, granite-solid and*—

Dex pulls the slab of chub out of my mouth. It's not over for either of us, though. I realize quite quickly that he has the entire evening planned and rattles off, "Has a guy ever sucked on your pole, dude?"

"Suck? … Pole?" I'm delirious.

The Apalli native snickers, "I didn't think so," and immediately places fingers around the joint between my legs and lowers his lips to the assisting-shaft.

It's the suck job of a lifetime as his tongue works cockhead and his lips fall gently and soothingly to my furry guy-balls. The sound of Dex's slurping echoes within the room, taunts my ears, causes me to blackout for just a brief second or two, with utter exhilaration, leaving me feel as I'm stranded with him on Mount Apalli, where the population is two, and the odds of us getting it on is better than good.

I push him off me, contacting my palms to his hulking shoulders. If he doesn't extract his tongue and lips from my private part, I'll explode a creamy treat into his fiery mouth by accident.

"Get up," I moan, saving an evolved climax for later.

He listens. If Dex wants our intimacy to continue, he'll accomplish nothing less. After standing again, strumming our cocks with his busy hands, he says, "Not bad timing again, McCallen. It takes a surviving man to hold back his load." He strays from the bed and leaves me watch him fetch a condom and tiny tube of lube.

Immediately, I ask, "What's going on, guy?"

It's too late for a response and explanation. I feel warm goo on my ass and one of his fingers against the slip of gay-chute. The blond snow god instructs, "I have to warn you that this is going to hurt." No mights or maybes. It's a definite.

I can't respond. I'm still laying on my back and he already has my legs hoisted up on his shoulders. The heated ranger immediately places the tip of his mounting peak into the sliver of my boyhood, allowing my innocence to dissipate almost instantaneously. Terror blooms on my face as I promptly grit my teeth, begin to choke on saliva and the hard cock that begins to enter inside me.

"Two inches are already inside, guy … eight more to go."

He leaves no room for debate. Dex plunges four more inches into my never-touched ass, smiles in the clouds, grits his teeth together, pulls all of the inches out, presses eight more in, and confesses magically above me, "This is how I thought it would be with you, Cade."

Ten thick inches of lumber delves into my opened hole. The tiny cabin starts to spin around and around as Dex continues to pound me. His massive pole sinks into my sliver of tightness with a systematic rhythm. I become mesmerized by his weight as he splits me into two, equal parts. My mind drifts through snow and around rock as if we are skiing down Mount Apalli again, man with man, man inside man, flushing and whizzing, breaking aerodynamic records. The sexual connection between us utterly spine-jolting and conducive. Our smooth embrace is nothing less than a test of masculine rank, strength between men. It is energy that prompts explosions and breath-clenching fury. It is needed and derived sex between two attracted and attractive men— completely cock-driven!

He can't help himself anymore. Dex is a potent and competitive man, but still gives into the pleasurable avalanche that is ready to spurt from his mountain piece. After what feels like an endless hour of pumping and thrusting into me, the plastic is unleashed from his McCallen-poker and it goes flying to the floor. Dex reaches down to his V-spot between stinging legs, and with both hands, toys his hardened ranger-puppet to burst a load of evening juice all over me, glazing my skin like snow covering Apalli. Remington states, "Bring it on, man ... Don't be shy."

"It's too late ... look what you did," I utter between clamped teeth. I'm so turned on by the ranger's glorified movements that it merely takes me two strokes on my pounder before spew circulates and drips over my chest like a cum-storm. Drop after drop of pearly white sap flushes out of my cock's head, garnishing my torso, spike-like nipples, and chin.

After my blow, Dex utters, "Looks like I taught you well, guy." He giggles mischievously above me, leans over me, kisses his cock to mine, and then extends his tongue to our freshly exposed drops of man-jizm, lapping me clean, coming up for air, whispering, "Just a boy ... Now a man."

There is one blanket and two naked men wrapped beneath its cottony niceness in front of the churning fire. Dex Remington holds me next to him, kisses my earlobe, the length of my neck, and asks, "It's about man and muscle don't you think?"

"Man and muscle," I whisper back.

"Like lust at first site?"

"Yes," I respond, kissing him back.

"Can I tell you something else, Cade?"

I nod my head with approval.

"I decided two things when you first showed up on my mountain."

"And what might they be?"

He cups me in his arms, shelters me, keeps me warm from the cold and biting wind outside. "One, you got the job right away. And two, I believed I found a new boyfriend almost instantly."

Shaking my head, I say back, "You have to pass a test to be my boyfriend, Dex."

The fire cracks as the wind purrs outside. "And what might that be, McCallen?"

I cup his semi-erect cock and stiffening balls into a hidden hand, and say, "Show me another rigorous challenge, dude."

Dex giggles. The tiny kisses to my neck tell me that by dawn I will learn everything I need to know about guy-with-guy activities, connections between men, homo-bliss. Snowblown.

ROBBY'S HOBBY

~ ~ ~

I was trespassing and watching Luke Hobby for weeks down on the docks without him knowing it. There was this little place where I hid—a private and obscure place beneath a San Francisco bridge—and I was left to grow hard and uncomfortable between my legs. As I peered at Hobby's massive size I felt ripples of sweat form all over my body, I watched him work bare-chested and sweaty on a privately owned boat called *All Mine*. As this deckhand tended to a twenty-four foot schooner along the Bay, I studied Hobby's yacht-sized body with its bronze and hairless chest, pointed nipples that shined like glass in the summer sun, ladder-like abs, thighs that were positively designed out of steel, and a face that said attractively delicious all over it. Hobby was the cause of the man-pole that was at attention and spewing out droplets of pre-sap between my legs. Hobby was my simple obsession and craving—something I needed for pleasure.

It was unreal what happened, and so quickly, an unexpected but fitting niceness between strangers. The guy spotted me under the bridge with my pants down as I rocked the meat between my legs, thrusting palms up and down on my inflated buoy. Quickly, I tried to run away from the scene but Hobby was too fast, had legs of power and a body that was charged with protein-induced testosterone. He yelled out, "Hey, you!" and bolted towards me, practically collapsed me to the ground, pinned me to earth, managed to almost press his nicely lined lips to mine. As I began to wrestle towards safety I felt his pecs and chest against my own, man gently pressed to man. His jean-covered cock rubbed against my bare one, causing a bliss-filled moment to bloom in my twenty-four year old world, allowing more droplets of spew to jet out of my bight and ...

He almost shoved his tongue directly down my throat, touched my goods, my ass, my back, but eventually managed to gently pick me up by the scuff of my neck—a mere seventeen feet from my hiding place, mind you. The dude spun me around in his firm but harmless grip, positioned me on the ground in front of his heavily breathing chest that I wanted to lap the bubbles of perspiration from.

Of course, he caused my eyes to stare into his brilliantly amber ones. Helplessly and erotically I became hypnotized at the tiny sliver of scar on his upper lip, an injury from his precious childhood, and was left to admire his somewhat deep nostrils that now flared with anger. The moment, as I stood half-naked before him, my shorts around my ankles, was intoxicating. I stayed unfailingly hard before him, found him to be sweet looking, more handsome than before, and *all mine*.

Hobby didn't move. He peered at the swollen beef between my legs, at my dangling balls of brown fur, and the line of hair that dragged from the V-section between my legs to my slick with sweat torso and nicely cut abs. Hobby, with all honesty, was into me, had liked what he saw. He admired my body with its tangible balls and cock, the dark hair lining my legs, and even my Bay-blue eyes. He liked me ... almost instantly, and was obsessed with me as I was fixated for him.

"What the fuck are you doing out here, guy?"

"Don't hurt me ... I'm harmless ... I'm just hooked on you."

"You're what?" Hobby looked quizzically strange by my comment.

I was honest though, and replied, "I'm hooked on you, dude … and you know it."

"I don't know what you're talking about. What's your name, anyway?"

"Robby Trance."

"Trance," he started, "you've gotten yourself into a fine mess. Do you know that?"

"I was just watching you."

"With your pants down?" He checked out my goods again. Carelessly eyed me up and down as afternoon food, he rubbed fingers across his mouth to catch saliva from his lips, perhaps overly-hungry for my skin.

I coyly smiled at him, shared a boy-next-door grin, nodded my head, and replied with skill, "You're something nice to look at, Luke Hobby, and you know it."

He stumbled across the concept that I knew his name. Hobby asked, "How do you know who I am?"

"That's not important."

"It is to me."

"Why do you want to know?" I was in no position to argue. I was smaller than him, boyishly hot and very attractive; someone who didn't need any scars on his face from Hobby's pounding.

Surprisingly, shockingly, and unexpectedly he looked to his left and right, found no one around, and touched me with his free hand. I felt his large fingertips roll against the top of my pointer. I listened to him breathe heavily with a sense of contentment as Hobby's fingers wrapped around my shaft and began to stroke it up and down in a playful manner, using the skin as if it were a toy. The water god licked his lips, kept his view on my rod and released the back of my neck, eventually cupping his other palm to my swinging ball-sack, enjoying his new find.

It was time to bolt, run for safety, and free myself from that awkward situation. I couldn't move, though. His hands were tantalizing my skin as a soft wind blew against our bodies. Hobby's touch was warm and soothing, caused me to grow another inch with playfulness. He, I realized in a quite stultified manner, was not about to hurt me, had enjoyed what I had to offer. And as our eyes connected and blended together, a trance forming between us, he offered, "Robby, you showed me yours, now let's go onto the boat so I can show you mine."

All Mine. It was beautifully elegant and enchanting. Hobby, because he wanted me on that day, desiring nothing less than a sultry obsession of man harbored to man, escorted me onto the schooner. And as he convinced me to go out into the Pacific—a vast plane of waving summery blues—the schooner's mast positioned all high and mighty, thick bull rope untied from two buoys, the boat released into the exultant waters, I saw him watching me, keeping his gaze concentrated on my good looks that he had easily surmised as strikingly model-like.

We floated out into the middle of the blue-blue world where there was no one to see or find us. Stranded in the Pacific, he meandered up to my side, pulled me against his skin, locked his lips to my neck, my check, and eventually my firm lips. Hobby cupped my khaki-covered goods, ground his hand into beam and balls, and caused me to grow hard again. He kissed my neck, pulled his hand away from me, and instructed in a nice manner, "I want to see *all* of you now."

I liked him, had fallen for him approximately three weeks before. I watched him stand in line at our bank, immediately found him appealing, followed him to his Jeep Wrangler, his apartment on Beckner Avenue, and eventually his place of employment along the bay. A part of me had somewhat been driven to enjoy his flesh as a visual comfort, a mere need for my man-survival. Of course, I listened to him, happy with the moment, ready to show him what I had to offer and what his skin was about to rub against. I removed

54

my T-shirt and shorts, stood on the deck of the schooner in my bare essentials, awaiting his own nakedness.

His constant gaze scaled my stuffed biceps and arms, my toned torso, thick thighs, and the mast-sized cock which dangled between my pulsating legs. The sailor approved of the beheld sight among the choppy waves, the sapphire blue bay, and a warm wind that was delicate against our chests, which kept both our sets of nipples erect. I felt his lips curl against my own as Hobby's exploring fingers grasped my extension of pick. After an exploding kiss between men, he pulled off, shared a masculine giggle, and supplied, "You're a hot guy, Trance. Now tell me what you want with me."

The words expelled from my mouth without any thought involved, "I want your ass and I intend to have it."

Charming Hobby asked, "Why is my ass so important to you?"

"Because it's the hottest I've ever seen."

Hobby used my comment as ammo for our shared company, immediately stripped out of his clothes, exposed a nine inch hard-on with cut cap and veins, and suggested, "Let's stop the bullshit and get to the point, Trance."

I directed my gaze down to my steeping and muscular pole and responded, "The point's right here, dude. What do you plan on doing with it?"

Hobby licked his lips and laughed, "What every horny guy wants to do with a fag's flag."

The upper deck was hard on my knees as his condom-covered bar clung to the back of my throat. Hobby rocked his wood into my mouth, kept palms leashed to my shoulders, pushed into me triumphantly, pulled out, pushed into me again, and praised my mouth-hole by saying, "Suck on it hard, Trance. If this is what you want, then take every last inch of it."

I choked on his plank, mounted to it with hunger and fortified desire. As the compulsive inches grazed my throat I moved palms up and over his pectorals, found his firm nipples, and squeezed both with utter hardening joy. Between my legs—a devise for him that was possibly ready to burst a load of man-chow to the schooner's boards—I felt tingles of sexual bliss echo through my swollen mass of handy protein.

Hobby—a man of writhing and bucking motion above me—wept and groaned with our mouth-to-cock connection. Hobby, prosaically numbed with guy-satisfaction, humped my oral insides constructively, repeatedly, and cyclically, ready to blow his load into the condom, searching out pleasure to his fullest capacity.

Of course, I teased him, pulled my mouth and finger off and away from his pent desires. And quite playfully I stated, while rising from the stern's boards, "Give me one good reason why I shouldn't buck your ass, Hobby?"

Luke Hobby looked at me with a bedazzled smile, reached between my legs for the hard goods that would make him feel as a rolling undertow had taken over his unyielding buttocks, and coached me on by uttering, "My ass is all yours, Trance … Don't let me down."

As *All Mine* rocked to and fro on the Pacific's choppy waters, I positioned my swelled oar between Hobby's opened legs. He laid on his back with his own scull stiff against his abdominal, its head glistening with excited man-sap at the tip. Hobby navigated his view down and along his sculpted hull, directed me efficiently, "It's time to slip your cruiser into my harbor, Trance. I can't wait any longer. Do your thing."

Willfully I obliged his craving, held the eight inches of steamy weight in my right hand, poked the top of my plastic-covered rigger against his pink slip, and began to anchor myself to Hobby like a good boy.

Hobby immediately started to groan as one inch of my humping tool opened him up. His chest rose and fell with my movement as the veined rod suctioned to his manly fiber, inch after pulsating inch. The deckhand's majestic eyes rolled into the back of his head as his teeth locked together. With his massive palms clamped to my hips, I watched pearl-like droplets of spew drip out of his Robby-teaser and glaze his supine looking chest where ladder-like abs constructed the perfect torso.

While selfishly pushing his legs apart, attempting to find Hobby's gay-soul, I manipulated and guided my spear into his warm and hairless crack, rocking steadily inside him like the boyfriend that he would end up keeping after that day, becoming overly greedy for me again and again. Beneath my infiltrating actions, my throbbing lust, and wavering delight above him, Hobby begged harmoniously for more of my sturdy inches to cause a tempest of pleasure to continue manipulating his accessible chute. Over and over again he called up to me, "Robby, nail me! ... Nail me hard! ... Nail me to the boards!"

I wouldn't let him down; I wouldn't let his cock down. Speedily and completely transfixed to his muscled body—a plateau of ripples and musky sweat, a splendid smile of preoccupied ecstasy and thirst smeared over his handsome face—my flagstaff worked diligently in and out of his shipping yard. I desired Luke Hobby like no other man, found him to be edible and fuckable; the ultimate sex-ride, a found obsession in my homo-world—simply mine. And without hurting him, rather pleasing my Bay-find with ripples and inches of packed lust, I heatedly throttled all of his insides with my hard mass, and caused his erect gear to bounce up and down against his solid chest. With my motion his cockhead kept dipping into the pre-ooze that had squirted onto his tanned plain of muscles lining his stomach. The erection rose slightly, fell again into the pool of bittersweet goo—a compulsive act of guy-play between us that had almost caused both of our steamy bodies to simultaneously orgasm and quiver gayly, extinguishing accumulated loads.

Smack ... smack ... smacking my pelvic bone to his backside, my inches of boner prompting Hobby to come at any second, his compulsive groaning and moaning became louder and louder, I called down to him with utter chaos, "Let's bring it home, guy ... You and me ... together."

He obliged with necessary comfort and allowed me to wrap a hand around the firm length of his strumming and stinging stick. Luke Hobby went to town on my hand, bucking wildly into my grasp, pushing his hips upwards as my pipe rolled in and out of him. He gulped for air, grew rosy in the cheeks, became flustered as if convulsing with our movements. Hobby humped my hand with exquisite beauty and desire as I continued to control his tight ass with entering and exiting meat. I watched him move steadily up and down with me, both of us becoming overheated, both of us saturated with perspiration. We began to moan together, in harmony, with turbulence and mere pleasure rolling through our bodies.

Immediately, I yanked my cock from his ass, pulled the condom free and tossed it to the schooner's deck. In the most steadfast manner between new lovers, I felt Hobby's fist around my pole, working meat up and down, willed to blow my juice off onto his smoothly lined chest.

"Now, Trance! … Do it now!"

We were incapable of holding back any longer. Hypnotically embraced by each other, we had every intention of blowing our loads with full-throttled force, decorating abs, nipples and navels. The first bubbles of spew rocketed out of our spigots and burned torsos, mixed with perspiration and heated longing. I murmured above him, flung my head back, felt my neck cords tighten, and extinguished my burst onto his skin. We were synchronized companions who gagged for air, howled in anticipation of our loads bursting everywhere, both captivated by the enticing moment of a heated connection of lust between us.

Hobby, I knew, carried out the same grunting noises in a wild and ferocious manner. While gritting his teeth, he breathed emphatically, "It's all yours, Trance … You finally have what you want. Every bit of it is yours." Pivoting fists against his rod, humping upwards, Hobby was a storm beneath me that worked his beef until his cream spiraled out of his shooter and glazed my pulsating skin. He was overcome with heavy breathing, satisfaction, and a waterfall of jizm that flushed out his cock until there was not a single drop left. Hobby was fulfilled now, completely spent.

On the hard boards of *All Mine*, clinging together, man on top of man, we kissed for the longest time and giggled like boys. Eventually, the sailor pulled away from my embrace, chanted crazily at me, "What do you want with me now, Trance?"

I rolled against his sticky body, clung to him, and recited back with care and need, "I'll come up with something … now that you're Robby's Hobby."

BREAKFAST IN BED

~ ~ ~

I own a cafe down on Abner Street called Acompanar. It's Saturday morning and I'm sleeping in, letting the management handle the place. I hear the door open to the townhouse in the big city, become more startled than ever. Someone's breaking in, invading my home. There's a mirror on the other side of the room. I look from myself (Puerto Rican brown hair, buffed bod, twenty-eight year old shimmering brown eyes) to the television, the closed and unlocked door, and then to the bat that sits beside my boyfriendless bed. I damn myself because I haven't turned on the security system the night before. There are whispers that mix together downstairs; noisy noises that are not of the caliber of a burglar. I try quickly to think who has the house keys: plumber and ex-lover (Carlos), mother (Martha Downy), and best friend (Tommy Payne). The voices aren't recognizable, though. The trespassers are clamorous and clumsy, and eventually move up the creaky stairs in what sounds to be a rally of sorts. They pound on the wooden door, turn the bedroom's doorknob and . . .

"Good morning, Paul Downy! . . . Today is your breakfast in bed!" It's Ivan Meadows, the hottest of hotties (white spiked hair, wrestler-tight body, piercing blue eyes, gold earring hoops in both ears, twenty-nine years old, popping muscles on arms, legs, and chest) of the morning TV hit cooking show *Breakfast in Bed!* He's a spectacular muscled bulk of chef in the city who stands in my bedroom, stares at my white sheets, silk pillows, and a naked me as I lay in bed. A tent shows off my semi-erect cock that has kept me company all morning because of a tasty dream filled with three men in a bathroom and a sex scene that is very similar to that in a Falcon movie.

I wonder what the hell is going on and see adorably plain Tommy Payne behind Ivan Meadows. Tommy is smiling from cheek to cheek like a little boy, up to no good, having had this adventure planned for me.

As a cameraman zooms his camera around the room, eventually focusing on delicious Ivan Meadows as he climbs into bed with me, Ivan presses his massive and manly hand against my dark and naked chest, chants into my ear in a bubbly manner, "Rise and shine, sleepy god. Ivan is here to fix you the most splendid breakfast." He winks at me and the camera, smiles an honestly infiltrating gleeful smile that could easily knock every guy off his feet.

I'm speechless and hard, try to cover up my man-splinter under the sheets.

As he begins to exit the bed, moving across the morning sheets in a slow manner, our eyes connect. Ivan runs a finger across one of my tan and hard nipples, between my legs. He makes contact with my erection, but neither of us respond, except for eyes that blend and melt together. Slowly he glides across my morning wood, pulls away, and then smiles at the camera again in his manly divine manner.

"Up-up, Paul!" Ivan coaches, stands at the corner of the bed. He then demands that everyone leave, that he will prep me on what the show has to offer this morning.

I want the cameraman to zoom in on my muscled meat that is standing up-right between my legs before he leaves, because I wish to sport my erection to all the viewers in the city so I end up with a Saturday night date with a needed and hot guy. And another sliver of my nicely designed body of twenty-eight years old merely wishes to settle back in the sheets, grab my long cock and begin to stroke it off like a porn star for *Breakfast in Bed*.

But it is Ivan who yells, "Out everyone! Out! I need to prep Paul on everything."

The cameraman and cutesie Tommy vanish. I'm left with Ivan in the room, but he doesn't prep me. He closes the door, locks it, and then spins around to the bed. Ivan smiles again, says in his charming manner, "You are way too hot. I promise we won't show the city your cock, although I'd like to." He gently tugs on the silk sheet that hides my seven inch boner, teasing me. Our eyes connect with some questionable and fiery intoxication or gluelike substance between two desiring men that leaves me believe that becoming destined within his bulking arms is meant to be. He glares at me with a thickness that allows my pre-oozing shaft to jump slightly, leaving Ivan smile with a sense of pure satisfaction, perhaps even greed that I will emphatically become his.

I smile back, speechless and hard.

And then our connection merely passes, like maybe seventy percent of the taken men I have met. He vanishes, closing the door behind him, and allows me to stare down at my ready-to-blow veined slab of Ivan-tease between my throbbing and tight thighs as I lift the sheet and think: *Ivan is delicious*.

Ivan's television show is an hour long, and about forty minutes into it--camera running--I am looking like a superstar in my bed, waiting for Ivan, Tommy, and the cameraman to return. My nipples are hard and perky looking, and my eyes are wide awake. I've spent a dozen or more minutes fixing my dark hair, allowing that perfect tuft to hang up in the front that makes me look six years younger. I decide to stay naked under the sheets, just in case Ivan decides to slip under the covers with me in front of the camera--a common tease on his show that drives his viewers into states of drooling envy--and share his cooked breakfast with me, adding shock to the moment. I'm ready now to be the bedridden and hungry victim on *Breakfast in Bed*.

Outside the closed door I can hear Ivan whispering to his watching fans, "Paul is just going to love this. Shhhhhh . . ." Then the door to my bedroom opens and it's Ivan who slips gingerly to the side of my bed, carrying a tray of fresh foodies. He places the tray over my middle, says to me, "It's time for breakfast in bed, my friend." Something he says to all of his morning friends and viewers.

Tommy Payne is in the room with the cameraman. He winks at me and smiles, informing me that I look hot and dazzled.

There are tiny slivers of French toast filled with Philly cream cheese and strawberry preserves on the tray; each sliver has been delicately dipped in cinnamon, egg, and honey, then fried in ground corn flakes. A French roasted cup of coffee with mocha sits on a Noritake china saucer. There's egg strata too, and what smells to be fresh pineapple-orange juice beside a dainty cup of newly sliced fruit of kiwi and cantaloupe. And to top off the breakfast with sweet delight, there is another tiny, china plate with six vanilla flavored almond balls for those breakfasters who aren't watching their waistlines. My stomach groans with need at the sight of the food as I smile into the camera, and can't wait to dig in.

The cameraman scans his camera over the delicious foodies on the golden tray, obtaining a shot of my rippled torso, which is a slight turn-on for me, since I've always wanted to be in movies. Ivan advances into the sheets with me then, his leg touching mine, his hip slipping against my bare and hard one. He says rather festively, "Could you just die with all these wonders?"

63

I don't know if he's talking about the great food or all the pumped parts of my body that he seems to glide against, but answer him by uttering a happy, "Yes."

He rattles off what's on the golden tray to remind all of the viewers again. One of his hands slips under the covers in a discreet manner. The only one who really knows that he carries this motion out is me, which leaves me to comprehend that Ivan is playful and knows that I'm naked. His searching and finding fingers reach between the V-split of my legs and he caresses my white, almond balls with a sense of breakfasting delight. He turns to me then with an edible smile, asks in a pleasant and cheerful manner as he rolls fingers over soft, clean shaven balls, "Shall we eat, Paul?"

"Absolutely," I whisper back, show off my smile to the camera. It takes everything I can to prevent my chiseled body to lean into Ivan's glorious one and share a morning kiss with him on camera. I hold back though, take the golden fork that he offers me, and begin to munch on his prepared meal with delight and ecstasy.

He strokes my balls with skill and grace under the tray and silk sheet. Ivan finds the slit of my ass between hard legs and caresses it gently as he pushes French toast into my mouth. He cuts into his egg strata and laughs into the camera, feeds me, asks if I'm enjoying myself.

I nod my head, feel my splintering man-pole beneath the tray rise to the occasion. I'm ready for my debut performance in adult films if Tommy would only step forward and take the food tray away, allowing my lips to find Ivan's hot body, and mesh like two deep-seeded morning lovers in front of the rolling camera.

It's Ivan who teases me, though. He presses fingers against my ass-slit, finds my ball-sack and plays with it. Eventually his roaming fingers reach the stem of my hardened cock underneath the tray. He rolls tips slowly up and down my pulsating shaft, teasing its bulbous head and veins.

"Yeah, that's good," I whisper of the food and Ivan's playfulness under the sheet.

"You really like it?" He asks.

My mouth is empty. I smile and nod my head as his fingers trail my monster-meat under the golden tray, mouth rather clumsily, trying to groan and moan with his pleasurable hands, but knowing that I can't because of the camera and audience, "The best."

There's a stream of cock-juice that erupts under the tray from his teasing fingers. Pre-cum leaks out the spitter-hole on my bedroom pleaser and it layers Ivan's fingers. He gently pulls the fingers out from under the sheet and quickly slips two of them into his mouth so the camera really can't tell what's on them. He moans with pleasure, swallows, cleans up his hands with his napkin, which really hides any leftover cum that may be on his skin, and chants to me, "You just can't get enough of this greatness." His intoxicating and lavish eyes flash at the camera next. He says something about seeing the audience next time on *Breakfast in Bed*, that they too could be on his show, and to watch out whose popping into their bedrooms at any shared time. He thanks me, thanks the audience, says something corny like, "Until we meet again," raises his coffee, washes down my spew. Ivan then says, "See you next time in bed," as he reaches for one of the almond balls and plops the breakfast dessert into his mouth.

The camera is off, but I still have a hard-on under the tray. Ivan turns to the cameraman and thanks him. The cameraman leaves, brushing past my friend Tommy. Tommy says rather pleasantly, with an infiltrating smile that allows him to be young and sweet, "I think I should leave you two alone." Maybe he knows about Ivan's antics under the sheet, or maybe he doesn't; Tommy's really too generous to say.

The pompous side of me determines quite quickly that hot Ivan and I will get it on. We will flip a coin to see who's getting done, or who's going to suck whom. Or, we will merely wrestle or kiss or damage each other with playful pats, allowing our bodies to simply mold together, twist and grind, until cum pops out of our ribbed rods and flies around my bedroom, decorating the walls.

Instead, he smiles, leans into me, kisses me on my cheek, "Nice job this morning. With a body like yours I'll get my ratings up."

I am stunned. My heart falls and my inflated cock tumbles with it. I merely gawk at Ivan as he climbs out of bed. I expect other items to *get up* instead of his ratings. But Ivan has no intentions of staying. "You're leaving?"

He's at the bedroom door, nods his head. "I have to. I'm sorry. But don't forget who I am . . . and don't forget that I'll be back."

"You promise?" It sounds like we are in some kind of relationship between guy and guy, between boyfriendless men.

"Absolutely, Paul. You're for keeps, if that's okay?"

It's a question, not a sentence. I nod my head, beam a smile, feel as if I could die by the passion of the hottest guy in the world. "Yes . . . keeps," I whisper, still smiling.

"Then I'll see you later, but I won't tell you when."

I wait and wait and wait. It's the fucking longest wait in the world. It almost sounds petty to tell the truth, but in the end, I'm a firm believer that if you wait long enough, if you search in your contained heart and soul, and that place between your legs slightly vibrates when you finally meet the right guy . . . then it doesn't matter how long you wait.

It's Sunday morning and Acompanar is closed, which allots me enough time to dream of my body with Ivan's, both pressed together with sticky niceness, with man-charm and champagne and sweaty abs and thighs. I dream until I can't dream anymore, until the fluff of my mind wakes me up and I need coffee. Morning wood sprouts between my naked legs. The house feels hotter than hell, hotter than the Mojave Desert or . . .

I sit up in bed and wipe the sleepies out of my eyes with a fist. Someone is in the room with me. I can vaguely see the blurry figure on the opposite side of the room. He whispers my name, "Paul."

I half expect it to be Ivan Meadows, but it's not. Tommy sits in the room with me, tells me that something is expected of me. He tosses a blindfold my way, and says to put it on, and not to say a single thing.

Tommy drives me somewhere across town in nothing more than my boxers, makes a dozen or more turns and stops. I haven't a clue what time it is or where I'm at. Eventually he pulls me out of his Saab, leads me up three flights of steps where it is warm and cozy, and says, "I have to leave now. But before I go, I just want you to know that this guy really likes you, Paul. . . . Don't blow it."

And here I am, pulling the blindfold from my eyes, dropping it to a parquet floor. I'm in a masculine room where there is a large bed and reading chair, novels on shelves, and a desk. I can also see a tiny breakfast cart with a silver pot of French smelling coffee, cups, and a plate of warm looking croissants. I look around slowly and absorb the room, believe I am dreaming.

But suddenly reality takes shape, because I feel someone behind me whispering into my ear, "Good morning, Paul . . . I hope I haven't startled you?"

I turn around and face a smiling, chiseled and perfectly sweet looking Ivan. He wears navy blue boxer-briefs that show-off an escalating package. A nipple ring dangles on his right, golden pec. His body looks like he works out four times a week, which has ultimately produced tight abs, bubbled arms, and leg muscles like vice grips. He smells of Ivory soap as he pulls me hard to his slender and pumped chest, leaving me unable to answer. And with severity, he kisses my mouth with his tongue and lips, allows me to half lose my balance, or half fall into a dreamy state of bliss and morning confusion. And he wastes no time, Ivan reaches for my meaty slab of guy inside my boxers, begins to roll fingers up and down on it. He pulls away from my mouth and says rather quickly, "I'm sorry about yesterday. I didn't mean to run off like that."

It doesn't matter. Ivan is far too hot for something this absurd. "Bygones," I whisper.

He chuckles, takes me hard into his arms, digs his teeth into my neck and shoulder, down to one nipple and then the slick and hard abs on my chest, holding me tightly within his hands.

I groan above him as he slips over my erect, eight inch cock, playing with its pulsing head with busy tongue. He laps up man-goo in his mouth, pinches my nipples with one of his free hands, breathes heavily over me, sucking on my meat-pole with a sense of pure ravage.

I run my hands through his icy hair, over his triceps, down his chest. I touch his hard skin on his pecs, feel the muscular V in his neck, breathe wickedly hard above him, groaning and feeling misplaced in the morning.

He pulls off of my swelled cock before a preconceived action takes place and I shoot cum into his mouth. And gentleman Ivan stands then, whispers, "There's something I need you to do."

I follow him to the front of the bed, hand-in-hand. The breakfast tray is to our right, the writing desk is to our left. "What?" I answer in a codependent manner.

He leans over the bed then, places palms on his navy, muffed sheets. "Pull my shorts down first."

I listen carefully to his instruction. His ass is the sweetest thing I have ever seen. Large, clean-shaven balls dangle between the crevice of his spread legs. I stare at the thin line of dick-need and say, "What's next?"

"Breakfast, of course."

He tells me there are condoms in the desk drawer, and to help myself. I'm back at the ass-site within a couple of seconds, slip the condom over my veined Ivan-humper, and ask him rather innocently, "Do you want half or whole milk

68

this morning?" before I position my hard, pulsating chute-plunger against his eye-opening man niceness.

He looks over his right shoulder and laughs, "Let's have the whole thing."

I listen again, hold onto his right hip with one hand, and guide my erection into place, pushing two inches of solid meat into him, then three, four, six, eight . . .

He moans beneath me, backs into the man-splitter. Ivan's palms are red from pushing into the bed. I reach around his steady hips with my free hand and find his cock; the hardest and longest (nine or so inches) of muscled guy-rod that I have ever touched. I begin to rock inside him, to and fro, while playing with cock, rolling fingers up and down on his shaft, feeling pressure build within him as I rip into his backside hard and harder, listening to him groan and cough slightly with the impaling slab of new boyfriend that's tightly locked into his ass.

He groans, "Harder," once.

I pull my splinter out and jab it into him with a turbulent power. Do it again, then again. One of my hands is still wrapped around his cock, working it, as my other hand holds onto his hip, possibly digging fingertips into his flesh for stability.

We rock back and forth like it is meant to be, like we are making a porno film for our eyes only. I slam everything into him that I can, feel as if I can explode into the plastic that separates us. My fingers touch the curves and lines in his cock, feel pre-cum surface at the bulb-head of his meat-demon as he thrusts it into my hand. Our motions are like a morning recipe: a pinch here, a taste of salt there, man-sweetness layering us together. We moan together, like men who are intended to groan, like men who have sexually satisfied many, but not with this expertise, this concoction of fleshy-baked niceness.

"I'm gonna pop," Ivan utters beneath me. His ass is the tightest in the world, a monument of my kindest affection.

"Me too," I roar pleasantly, chuckling behind his spread and hunched over splayed back.

"Let's blow, man. Okay?"

I pull out of him and rip the condom off quickly. He's already on the bed, facing me on his knees, holding his meat within one hand, balancing his weight with the other. Ivan's body is slicked with morning sweet-sweat, with ripples and hard lines. He whispers with a wide grin, "Two man-Danishes to go, please."

I climb up on the bed and face him on my knees, hold my Ivan-sausage in my right hand. "Let's do it," I whisper, "just like you want it."

And we blow, together, pumping our meats with hard fists, sweating on the bed, flushing white morning jism out of our hardened flag-cocks, thrashing spew against each other's skin, decorating abs and nipples and shoulders and noses and foreheads and cheeks and thighs and hips with a liquid that is the color of Ivan's hair. We blow our loads with impassive groans and pulsating rods as our hands move up and down, as our eyes stay wide to watch each other get off. Spew jets everywhere, covering us, layering our skin with a sweetness that is impeccable and world class, allowing us to eventually become spent together.

We lay together afterwards, body against body. He licks droplets of cum off my nipples and abs. Ivan calls it breakfast in bed.

I whisper to him, "You done yet?"

He comes up for air, glares at me with his piercing eyes, "Never. You're here for life. I want to make breakfast for you every morning. Would that be a problem, Paul?"

I laugh at that, allow him to lick me clean as he dabs his tongue against my silky and salty skin, prompting me to brush fingers through his hair, and to think: *He's a spectacular muscled bulk of chef . . . who has completely found me edible . . . and has fallen for me.*

HECTOR'S NECTAR

~ ~ ~

The Georgia heat is bothersome. I'm on my break, bare-chested and laying on the ground with palms locked behind head as a pillow. I'm daydreaming and half-asleep under a peach tree. As sunbeams ski through the leaves and the open spaces between the peaches I think about: men swimming, chests slick with river water, nipples taught, smooth legs, diving … coming up for air.

Hector Fast (sweet dark skin, California-blue eyes, rippled stomach, bleached-blonde hair, bulging arms, perfect teeth, twenty-six year old body, and just about enough charm to make you drop your pants upon immediately gazing at him) has been climbing and hanging in the peach tree like a chimpanzee for the past ten minutes.

"Hector Fast, what are you doing, dude?" I call up to him, eyes still closed. We work for Analysis Reach, a company that collects data on fruit products. Our jobs are quite complex—not really, but it sounds good. We work in fruit fields, mostly in Georgia, and measure fruit, taste it, analyze skin textures, sizes, and make other various calculations on the world's produce. Our finds are sent to state agriculture labs that are enforced by the government. It's all about standards for the public ... safety, too.

Right now, we're breaking. We've just finished lunch and decide to rest in the warm shade for just a few minutes.

Hector answers me, "Nothing, Jance ... really." His voice is raspy, heated, and sexy as he begins to grunt. I think he's stretching or something, doing exercises in the hulking peach tree, carrying out pull-ups with pulsating biceps that are sexy-sweaty, or merely hanging from a stiff branch, palms cocked behind him, pulling his body against gravity, up and up and up, toning his shimmering abs and leg muscles, working out.

"Stop your grunting, man ... you're going to turn me on," I joke.

His menial groaning becomes louder at Mason Grove, though. Hector's breathing increases, louder and more vibrant. As seconds pass, I hear him whisper intoxicatingly, "Jance Sellact, here it comes ... Sorry, dude, I couldn't keep it in."

To my utter, scandalous, and shocking surprise, I feel droplets of warm liquid fall to my lips and chin, all over my cheeks, and down along the slope of my tight neck-cords. Some of the sweet smelling liquid falls into my mouth as Hector's grunting turns into a hollow and pleasing moan. The taste of the liquid is bittersweet, gooey, and sticky. Immediately I sit up, open chocolate colored eyes, look northward bound in the tree, and see Hector hanging upside down from a thick limb. Before I can utter any type of shocking reply, I feel more of the drops of wet-astonishment fall to my ladder-shaped abs, nipples, and shoulders. The liquid is hot and burning against my skin, perfectly clingy. "Hector, what in the hell are you doing?"

He's beautiful in the tree: white hair hanging down, cut abs, peach-like balls that are lightly fuzzy, triangle-spot of blonde pubic hair, and perfect hands working on ten inches of veined and uncut cock. Hector Fast is naked and stinging in the tree, dangling by his legs that are bent over the peach

72

tree's limb. His face is shiny-red-brown, bears puffed cheeks, wide eyes, blowing the last of his load down and over my body, showering me with man-goo, decorating my skin and face, shooting a steamy-warm load of man-burst that is stinging-hot.

The dude takes a deep breath in, exhales, and exclaims, "I couldn't help myself, Jance ... I was up here thinking how hot you looked down there napping... how sweet your skin smelled ... and I just couldn't stop myself."

I'm sticky and wet, covered in his shoot, half-pissed out of my mind, and yet half-dazzled by the moment. "Stop jerking around, Hector, we've got work to finish out here."

He finishes stroking his branch and chants whimsically, "You need a vacation, Jance. Take a load off and join me, okay?"

"Hector, you're going to get us into deep shit if you don't stop these antics."

He used to be an award winning gymnast in high school and currently decides to partake in his skills by doing a flip off the branch and landing in front of me: bulky arms flex and curl into his perfectly designed sides, muscled and glistening legs pivot tightly together with feet, chest firms up as upper body tucks into lower torso, all body parts carrying out the perfect spin. With an abundance of expert movements, Fast lands in the dust directly in front of me, and immediately laughs, "At some point in your youth, Jance, you're going to have to remove that angry tree from your ass."

I'm not amused, and bitch back, "And what else am I supposed to do, kiss your ass all the way to the unemployment office when we get fired?"

There are no towels available in the grove. No handy wipes. Nothing to clean up with. As my skin glows with Hector-spew he tries to win me over by saying, "I'll take care of you, Jance ... no need to worry." And to my shocking, astonishing, and utter surprise, Hector moves up to me, slightly lowers his head, and begins to lap up his sweet juice from both nipples.

I twirl above him as he sucks on my nipples and waving abs. Hector's pointed tongue dives at my neck and chin, my cheeks and nose, eventually finding my mouth, lapping up his own goods, devouring the goo, hungry for his own grove-load. Obsessed with me, watching me for weeks in the assortment of peach groves that we have visited together, relishing my man-goods (perfectly trim torso, mannish skin that is sweetly soft, inflated biceps, bursting package between muscular legs, and tapered-sliver of mouth), and craving nothing less than my company, Hector pushes his tongue deep and deeper into my mouth, leaving me feel bemused or light-headed, lost without directions in Georgia. Fast pulls out of my mouth and uses my skin with his tongue, desiring me, tasting and testing me as if I am a needed fruit, bathing his thirst in my afternoon pours as he becomes obedient to my skin, leaving me unabated and half-swollen between legs.

I push him away and explain, "Not here ... not now. Someone will catch us."

The palmolgist generously slips his hand into my khaki shorts and cups my fuzzy fruits. He says rather implicitly, adoring me, "Maybe that wouldn't be so bad, Jance."

"We'll get fired."

And he adds something crazy, but cozy, "As long as we're together, that's all I care about."

Serenely I push him away by placing a palm against his slick chest. He wants my skin more than anything, like how a fruit fly desires the peaches. I tease Hector as he carries out his sweet inspection of my body, licking his lips, eyeing me up and down in a heavy and heated manner. He wants to get caught in a compromised position with me, finds it a total turn on. Hector is mad for me, every inch and limb, every word I breathe, utter, or complain. He is a carnivore of desire, and I am nothing less than his grove pet with a dashing smile and princely looks.

"Put your clothes back on, Hector."

He's too dazzled by me to carry out such a menial act. He's too into me. The guy wants me so bad, finds me arrogantly sexy and mature, that he won't listen to instructions. "Take your shorts off for me, Jance."

I won't listen to him. He won't have me. The golden boy toys with my erotic state, causes shimmers of ecstasy to wiggle up my spine, through the growing trunk between my legs. I will not share with him how he drives me mad, or how handsome he is, cute and boyish, playful and sinister-sweet. I can't let Hector know of my secret lust for him, that his mischievous and sexual actions drive me crazy and hard.

The grove is warm and sweet smelling. Honeybees dance around bodies as unused clipboards lay in the sun with Bic pens nearby. It's sugary Hector who says, "You're playing hard to get, Jance."

I shake my head, "Really, I'm not … we have work to do. According to our schedule we have three more groves waiting for us today."

"And I'm waiting for you to loosen up." Hector reaches around me, his forearm brushing against my left cheek, and grasps a Romantic peach from a thin branch. The cutie positions the peach in front of my lips, and instructs, "Time to work, Jance, take a taste test."

It's my job detailing the taste of the grove's product, a file that will be forwarded to and reviewed by our immediate boss at Analysis Reach. With Hector holding the peach in front of me, I take a bite of the fruit, chew it up, swirl it around inside my mouth, take mental notes (sweet and smooth, grade-A taste, soft skin that is thin, a fleshy and very romantic fiber that is not chewy but refreshing), and swallow. Peach juice carelessly drips out the right corner of my mouth. Fast, to my mind-numbing likeness, takes his right palm, busies two fingers against my lips and right cheek, and swabs up the orange-pink colored juice. And out of mere need or heightening desire, he moves the fingers to his own mouth, and begins to suck on them in a timely, guy-appropriate, and stimulating manner.

He's out of control, still risky, still preoccupied with the notion of seducing me, and using my skin and the current position of the peach against my lips. Devious Hector squeezes the peach with the force of pressed-together fingers, prompting fruit juice to dribble on my lower lip and chin. The stream of juice drips down the length of my neck, between sun-baked pecs, and continues south over my chain of abs, falling and dripping into my khaki shorts, deeper and deeper. The boy-like sap runs along the line of treasure hair beneath navel, into the patch of V-shaped pubes above stem of cock, along the silky curves of my drooping balls, and eventually down the length of my right, inner thigh, clinging to my heated skin.

My God ... he uses me in a handy manner, carrying out this act on purpose, driving me mad, causing me to enjoy the moment with utter, stimulating bliss. I am left to weep for him, the seduced coworker, manipulated, dazzled ... and hard.

He smolderingly asks, "You like it, Jance, don't you?" and takes his right hand, gently cups my newly derived erection and balls, and caresses them with a circular movement.

I quiver, breaking down, unable to pent off my hungry appetite for him. I imagine he will use me right in the grove, man pressed against man, Jance weak and fragile and hanging from a branch, trembling erratically, and Hector inside him, molding to him, invading my property, trespassing, and eating me up whole, leaving me spent and sexually catatonic ... numb.

"You'll have to give into my wants soon."

I'm barely capable of shaking my head, but do. "You'll have to work harder, Hector ... You don't have me yet."

My zipper is unzipped. My shorts are pulled down. He sees that I'm boxer-free and smiles at me, and inspects my goods, explaining, "I'm impressed with your portions, Jance. The state will like the figures I've found. Our report will be impeccable." Hector's steady fingers dabbles with the excess skin on my eight inches of erect tree. He toys with my fuzzy scrotum, hypnotizing me with his unwavering gaze.

"I'm not giving into you, Hector."

He laughs on knees, still playing with my balls, now watching the timber between my legs swing west to east like a temperate storm. "You already have." His tongue finds the peach-liquid on my skin, the tip of my uncut cockhead, the veins lining my rod, and the two balls swinging between firm legs.

I won't let him be right—it's not possible. I will not give in to his sexual means and throbbing, biting, pushing, pounding, and working devices. He won't have me because I'm a professional crop profiler, a fruit tester, handler, and specialist. He won't …

My god … he has me in his mouth, sucking on my skin, my rod, caressing my balls, pivoting me into dazzling, uncharted spins, causing me to grow hard and harder, bigger and stronger, like a peach tree, a heated man in the secret grove, eating me whole, relishing me, absorbing himself with my cultivated garden of delight, consuming my eight inches down his throat, sucking on me, testing me, and exploring my product with need, greed, and oral interest.

"What's happening?" I heavenly utter above him. "I'm shaking, Hector … quivering."

He is far too occupied to respond to my concern. Without much ado, without questioning the likeness of man attached to man in the peach grove, I feel a volcanic rush vibrate rhythmically throughout my body, having my hips thrash forward, bucking into the blonde's face and sucking mouth. With candor and utmost reverence, balancing myself from falling to the ground by his mouth-movement, digging heels into southern dust, I am compelled to do nothing more than to fire off a steeping and warm man-load into his mouth, cleansing Hector, feeding him, abating his craving for the time being, causing him to become exhausted and drained with my body and its delicious, masculine nectar.

Our sticky bodies are sealed together after he consumes my Jance-chow. Hector utters with a joyful and pleased smile after wiping his mouth with the back of his right arm, "I'm not done with you yet."

"You won't have me again."

He wants to kiss me; I pull away. "You don't think so, Jance?"

I shake my head, fend him off by pushing him away, all loveless and heartless, and respond rather rudely, "I know so, dude ... No way you're getting any closer to me. What's done is done ... over and finished. Let's get back to work."

Later in the day, after returning from Mason Grove, I'm sitting behind Mr. Boss's luxurious desk, called in for a meeting. The guy directly says to me across the desk, "Sellact, I heard you had an altercation with Hector yesterday at Mason Grove."

"An altercation?" I ask. Shit, what's he talking about ... altercation? Hector blew his load over me, licked me clean, and eventually sucked me off. There was no altercation. Next, I think: *How does he know about us? Who saw? What voyeuristic freak was in the grove watching our movements? I'm definitely in deep shit. Out of a job. Unemployed. Fired. Someone saw our man-action in the grove, turned us into Mr. Boss. God, what an awful day.*

Mr. Boss opens a drawer, tosses a stack of papers onto his desk and says, "None of your analysis matches. Hector's results are different from yours, Sellact, and ..." He rattles on and on about gathered facts at Mason Grove, and eventually instructs, "If you can't work with Fast, I can find someone who does."

"I can work with him." I reach for the stack of papers, review them quickly. Fast's results are higher on the scale than mine. Usually we meet in the middle with results, almost identically match. "You two make a good team, Jance … I don't understand your results. I always thought teaming you up together was a good idea. What happened out there?"

Am I turning red? Am I hard in my seat? Am I angry?

To cover my ass with Boss, I say bluntly, "Let me hook up with Fast and see what this about?"

Boss says, "Fine …. Get back out to that field and re-work your results."

I stand and reply, "Yes, Mr. Boss." I'm about to leave when Boss calls out my name from his desk. Quickly, I spin around, attempt a ludicrous and helpless smile, "Yes, sir?"

He points to me and adds in a gruff manner, "Get your head in the game, Sellact … Hector's one of our best … Don't let him down."

Don't let Hector down. How can I? Isn't he too cute and charming, simply delicious looking with his icy-blonde hair and tanned skin, his youth and niceness? Isn't he just edible? Of course I won't let Hector down.

We're out at Mason Grove again, a second time around. Data is collected and our figures are matching up. We're working together well. Compatible. I'm quiet and reserved, keep to myself, getting the job done. Hector senses my silence and questions, "Boss up your ass yesterday?"

"Something like that."

He takes one of the peaches off the trees and starts to eat it, bite by bite, swallows, teasing me.

"You're crazy," I say.

"You had it coming."

I plunge forward then, ready to strike him. The peach falls out of his hand and tumbles to the ground. I scare the shit out of the fag and he drops with the peach, losing his balance. Diving on top of him, we wrestle like champions, man against man, chests pressed together. Our noise is nothing less than what animals derive. Growling. Grunting. Our actions are brutal as my palms lock against his arms. Successfully I have Hector pinned to the ground, leaving me positioned overtop him. Our cocks greet and meet each other. Tense and erect nipples touch in the thick heat of summer as our eyes connect. I breathe him in slowly (a warm and fresh aroma of masculine-bliss, of sugar-sweet innocence that is very likeable) and mouth slowly, "I should pound you right now, Hector."

He turns his cheek for a blast, closes his eyes for my blow, and responds crazily, "Who's stopping you?"

"I don't mean it that way," I confess.

The peach turns his head to me again, smiles, and chatters, "In what way then, Jance?"

I kiss him like I have wanted to kiss him. A man's kiss that is heavy and thick, enchantingly rich. He is mine, I realize. No one else's—all mine. The kiss is real and rough, just right. I pull off and say, "I'm crazy for you, do you know that?"

He's too stunned to answer—I have him right where I want him.

Naked and heated, ripe and clean, Hector's palms are pressed against one of the peach tree limbs. He stands with his legs spread and ready for my consumption. The dude looks over his shoulder and explains, "Time for a data check, Jance."

I'm heated and ready, can't wait to dive into the blonde prince. With a Hot-Rod condom affixed to my pole, I slap Hector's right asscheek, listen to him yelp, and explain, "You really fucked up yesterday."

"And now you want to get even, right?"

I can't answer him because he's too hot, too handsome and perfect. Instead, I lean into him, press my slab of cock between his tight cheeks, bite at his neck, pull off, and ask euphorically, "Why do you like me so much, Fast?"

"You're the perfect type of guy for me."

"Like a perfect peach, right?"

He shakes his head. "Nope ... Better."

It's too late for explanations ... too late for sucking up in his boyishly cute manner. I slip the cock into him, spread him open, pivot three inches of fat slab into his hole, and cause him to groan and moan, wildly and emphatically.

"Don't stop," he utters.

"You've been terrible, Hector ... Take your payback." I find his guy-center for a quality performance and research his masculine insides, pounding him in a necessary manner, inch after feeding inch. He's the best fruit in the field, my test crop with just the right sweetness and a hint of tartness. I assess him wisely, indiscriminatingly and effectively. Hector becomes cultivated by my length, in and out, processed and analyzed by my inspection of eight throbbing inches that is delicious and hungry, needing to invade his grove and take his desire. Thrusting. Inducing. Impelling. Our pre-orgasmic stage is optimum ... A-class.

Hector Fast takes everything I have to offer, deeper and deeply, a façade of lust connects the two of our bodies together. He howls with my thrusting, pulverizing, and distinguished movements. Hector is fascinated by my rhythm and cock-driving performance, obtaining everything I have always wanted from him, consuming him, breathing with him, melding together as one, man rocking against man, fruit inspectors at work, and sweat-glistening needs becoming fulfilled—at last!

I manhandle his ass, unable to pent my load any longer, and press cock deeper and deeper into my find, blowing Jance-sap into condom, squirting into him wildly, uncontrollably, and purposefully. Crazily I grunt behind him, holding him close and closer, pushing him away, pulling him back onto my rod, continuously.

And Hector rides the thunderous storm, willingly. He's into me and my rod, my payback, a harvesting queen in our man-parade, a sweetly devoted peach-thing that is completely consumed—taken.

Now face to face, breathing heavily, we are predators together, eating off of each other, climaxing. After I blow my load, I inhabit his rod with my own right hand, wrapping it solidly around his vein. I think, *This is what it's all about ... Hector's nectar* and stand with my chest a few inches away from his. Slowly I work his cock up and down in a fierce manner. Hector's out of control, moaning and yelping like a wild dog, bucking his rod into my palm, breathing heavily and happily. He warns, "It's off the charts, dude ... you'd better stand back."

I'm willing to drown for him, I realize, liking him too much. As my fist and fingers pump his sword a few more times, a hot and fiery irrigation system erupts with liquid. Steamy field-jizm juts out and onto my chest. Droplets of Hector's goo clings to my burning skin, sticking to abs and naval, to nipples and shoulders, pleasing me. And as he shutters, laboring over connected tools, I confess richly, "I couldn't help myself ... I was thinking how hot you looked ... how sweet your skin smelled ... and I just couldn't stop myself."

His response is Romantic as he connects us together with a melting guy-kiss. Sweetly I rock his meat more and more, up and down, rhythmically, willing all of his creamy-white goo out, causing him to become spent and exhausted, mine for good, a boyfriend and lover ... simply mine.

STUDIO DUDE

~ ~ ~

I've died and gone to Guy-Heaven! Adorable, twenty-two year old me is really here! This can't be happening. Matthew Spider and I are actually in Studio Dude looking the best we've ever looked, shiny-fag-nice, feeling hot and cozy, tight all over, and just boyishly-perfect.

Rainbow lights flash and spin around on the club's ceiling and floor as luscious, dark-skinned Latino hunks dance around aluminum poles with mere triangular pieces of white latex covering up their bulging, semi-hard erections. Shirtless bartenders with steel-plated chests and decadent grins, with chiseled model-looks and hair to die for, buzz around, serving drinks from Queen Elizabethan trays. It's a help yourself kind of place, I've heard, and whisk a martini off one of the trays as Spider, my best bud, the star of this evening who has gotten us into this place called Studio Dude by the help of a friend of friend's one-night stand, lifts a Bud Light off the same tray. Spider is standing with his mouth open, droll hanging from his bottom lip, beer in right hand, looking foolishly delicious.

I coach him, "Dude, you're losing it. Pull yourself together."

"I can't believe we're here, Myth."

I stare at razor-edge cuties with glistening eyes and muscles out the wazoo, with gay-perfection at this absorbent nightlife that causes my growing cock to miraculously tingle like a gold dinner bell. "We're here, buddy, now go find some meat." I pat Spider on his tight little ass that is bubbly-right and set him free into Queerdom.

There are so many hot guys in the Southern California club. I feel bulbous asses graze my wrists and thighs as solid packages grind into my buttocks by accident. I feel men brush fingers nonchalantly against my firm nipples, my rigid pecs, pulling my tight, black T-shirt out of hard-to-get-into jeans, grazing fingers against that single line of blonde hair on my lower stomach, teasing me raw, causing me to grow hard and harder, forcing me to gulp the martini down in two diligent swigs. I hear: *I'm sorry, doll; excuse me, handsome; nice ass; gripping shirt; lead me into the bathroom and fuck me like a boy; you look naughty enough to blow a load with me, cowboy.* There's so much activity around me, men moving from south to north, from bar to dance floor, a busy freeway of melting men as Madonna blasts overhead, singing about music and people. So many men in such a little, buzzing place. Only at Studio Dude. It's a pleasure to be here.

There are superstars in the room: Clive Barker leans into Matt Damon and kisses his left cheek, whispers something into his ear that causes Matt's wide-white grin to boyishly appear, melting me; Ethan Hawke dances with Michael McConaughy, nipples to nipples, cigarettes in hand; porn stars, Tuck Johnson tongues Marcus Iron, deeply and erotically they have hands locked on each other's tight asses; John Edwards and Kenneth Cole, Ben Affleck and Tom Cruise, Robert Rodi and Chi Chi LaRue all spin conversation circles around and around with other famous guests, stunning me into silence and mouth-gaping awe.

Withdrawing me from my *Cinderella* dream-world, I hear a stranger whisper into my left ear from behind, one of his firm hands firmly tucked against my hip, "You're new around these grounds, aren't you?"

I spin around and see Prince Charming standing in front of me: green-blue eyes the color of the Indian Ocean; a perfectly crafted jaw; tiny lips; dimples planted into kissable cheeks; broad shoulders offering a muscular build; thick eyebrows like brushed ink; succulent cords in a strong neck. He pushes a masculine palm over his brown, buzzed head and shares a gallant smile with me that I prefer waking up to for the rest of my mortal life.

I'm ridiculously speechless. "Yes, I suppose."

"First time here in Studio Dude?" the stranger asks, looking awkwardly familiar with his glinting eyes.

I nod my head, feel half-embarrassed. "Yes. Can you tell?"

He leans into me, whispers into my ear, and grazes fingers to my bare chin in a tender manner, "It's okay ... there's nothing clumsy about you. You're carrying yourself well."

I see Spider over the stranger's right shoulder; he's dancing with two, shirtless guys, kissing both with his extended tongue, touching their private parts with his hands and stomach and ...

"What's your name, friend?" the stranger asks.

I draw my attention back to the interested stranger. "Bernard Mythington. Everyone calls me Myth."

"I like that, Myth. Do you want another drink?" He sees that my martini is very dry and smiles at me. "I'll get us both one, okay?" The stranger doesn't allow me to answer. He floats away into the thick crowd, becomes hidden by masculine bodies, buried underneath and between guy-flesh that can cause your cock to spurt a preload at any moment, unexpectedly.

He's not going to come back; it's in the gay handbook for ditching dudes that are duds: *tell the faggot loser that you're getting him a drink, and buzz away like a bumblebee; he'll get over it.* I stand and look around the club. Everything is exactly how I have imagined it: boys clinging to older men, lapping at hairy armpits; leather jackets slipping against firm chests; cocktails and cigarettes in every hand; hot Latinos mixing with white-skinned Russians; guys against guys, melding together in a sexual frenzy that is nothing less than dick-lifting.

"Did you miss me, Myth?"

I turn around and he's back. The stranger with no name. "Yeah. That didn't take you long."

He hands me one of the two martinis. "It never does when you know the bartender."

I take a sip of the dry martini, then another, and a third to top off the moment since this complete stranger has found me ... attractive company.

He takes a sip: lips part casually, moisten with niceness; white-perfect teeth clink crystal-like glassware. "Can I tell you something, Myth?"

"What's that?" I'm intrigued by him, growing firm in my Boxer Joes with his questionable way of carrying out this conversation.

The music is so loud, which forces him to lean into me, thick and clinging breath penetrating the soft skin on my neck, my earlobe, whispering, "It's a secret. You can't tell anyone. Promise?"

He's coming onto me. His free hand is cupped against my right ass-cheek. This is in the gay handbook for picking up hotties. The stranger wants a piece of my tight ass, whole or half, something. "I'm listening ... go ahead."

"I don't normally pick up guys like this, nor offer drinks. I'm the quiet type."

"You're far too cute to be the quiet type, Stranger. I don't believe you." Spider has taught me well in being hard-to-get.

"Believe me." The interloper of my evening looks sincere and honest, isn't handing me a line of bullshit out of a textbook for queenly readers; I can see it in the curves and mysteries of his Indian Ocean colored eyes.

"Convince me," I lean into him and whisper back, challenging him.

It's too late ... he kisses me, hard on the lips. Our mouths press together as the music and cigarette smoke drapes and wraps our bodies into a midnight cocoon. Our tongues meet as teeth click together accidentally. I feel weak and bubbly and half-drunk, becoming consumed by him, feeling the stranger's palm tighten on my ass, squeezing, kissing me again and again as a remix of Judy Garland's "Somewhere Over the Rainbow" rocks our man-against-man world.

The familiar stranger pulls off and says, "I have to make a pit stop, Myth. You'll be here when I get back, right?"

I smile at the stranger, see the twinkle in his eyes, his dashing grin and interest, and reply, "I promise again."

After the stranger heads off to take care of his business, Spider plows into me, is completely out of breath, has these wide cocoa colored eyes, and implores, "Man, we've got to get out of here right away!"

"Why?"

"The dancers are pissed at me or something. They we're saying how I was a dicktease and how they fucking hate guys who don't put out. I told them I wasn't that way that I was sorry, but they don't want to hear it because I think they've had too much to drink, Myth. They said something about a gang-bang and ..."

"Who?"

"The two dudes I was dancing with. I don't know their names."

Quickly, I look from Spider to the bathroom in the distance. The stranger isn't anywhere to be seen. My attention is abruptly drawn to the right as a Hercules-sized man with muscles from Earth to Pluto and back, rushes towards Spider with an outstretched, opened hand, ready to latch onto him, yelling, "You little teasing fucker!"

We bolt. There's nothing else to accomplish. Spider has been naughty (or not so naughty) and he and I must escape the club before we both get the shit kicked out of us by some drunken Hercules-type with a hard-on that needs to be pressed into virgin Spider.

And as Spider whisks me away, deep into the night, midnight at hand, I think of the stranger that I have fondly admired, finding myself curious for, and peculiarly inhabited by. Gone.

He's familiar, but I don't know him. The guy from the night before at Studio Dude is not a stranger at all, but I don't *personally* or *precisely* know him. There's something about his dimples in the delicate curves of his cheeks that causes me to believe I know him. I can't get him out of my mind. Stranger-world consumes me as I nap, eat, drink, and try to read.

It's afternoon and the phone rings, draws me out of my man-bliss world on Prince Street in my studio apartment. I pick it up the line on the third ring, say, "Hello."

It's Spider. "Hey, guy?"

He's ruined the previous night and I'm not too pleased with him, but say, "Hey," back.

"You want to see if we can get into Studio Dude again tonight?"

"Let it go," I encourage. "I need a rest from the club life, Spider. Maybe next time."

I shower to wash the stranger out of my mind, soap up my abs and stiff rocket, my pits and nicely designed thighs. I take forever in the shower, enjoying the spray, blocking out the stranger from Studio Dude.

Eventually, I escape the shower and begin to dry off, trot from the bathroom into my Parquet-floored studio near the bay windows that overlook busy Hollywood. And

88

standing here naked with a towel wrapped around my middle, with water droplets cascading down my muscular slimness, it hits me how I recognize the stranger from the night before. My eyes hang on a bookshelf filled with a variety of hardbacks over my Fung Shui positioned bed. On the shelf, I see books by Armistead Maupin, Felice Picano, and Stephen McCauley. Lastly, squinting eyes, and moving closer to the bookshelf, another one of my favorite writers is on the shelf-- the writer's name is Kris Brice; the stranger from last night.

"My god!" I pull down the best-selling novel called *Soul-Destiny* from the shelf and flip to the back cover, open it and see: green-blue eyes the color of the Indian Ocean; a perfectly crafted jaw; tiny lips; dimples planted into kissable cheeks; broad shoulders, thick eyebrows like brushed ink; succulent cords in a strong neck. "It's him ... It's really him! I've been kissed by Kris Brice."

I call Spider back about Kris Brice kissing me. Spider doesn't believe me, but when has Spider ever believed me about anything. I utter rapidly with loads of excitement, "Get us back into Studio Dude tonight! I'm on a mission, Spider. This is my destiny!"

The place is packed. Go-go dancers bounce around. Guys are almost flooring it's this steamy hot. I see Sandra Bernhardt, Jay Quinn, Daniel Baldwin, Ken Ryker, and so many other famous people, but not Kris Brice--he's nowhere to be found.

Saddened by near fatal crash with reality that Kris Brice is permanently out of my destiny-picture, reality settles into my gut and mind, deflating and grounding my queerly emotions, and I whisper softly, sullenly, "You'll never see him again, Myth. It's over."

I head back to my studio, abandoning Spider, left to my own devices.

Three days pass into four. I'm over Studio Dude and plan to never go back. I've found my own studio apartment as a

recluse. I'm reading *Gay Night Out: Looking for Prince Charming.*
I concentrate on one of the lines: *When the right guy comes along,
it will just happen on its own.*

"The hell it will!" I slam the book closed and toss it to
other end of the couch. "I'm never going to find Prince
Charming."

The doorbell to the studio buzzes, and I call out
through the echoic recluse, "Hold on a second!" I believe it's
Spider, begging to go out on the town, find a club to pursue,
or maybe return to Studio Dude.

The buzzer roars again. "Give me a fucking minute,
Spider, okay?"

What hits me is nothing less than a storm when I
open the apartment's door. It's a soft hit, directly in my
heart, warming up my veins and temperature. I open the
front door and whisper with surprise, "Dear god, look what
the wind blew in." I'm stunned and mesmerized, half-lean
into the door frame, staring wide-eyed with my mouth open
at the most handsome man in the world. Prince Charming
has arrived, and this evening he has a name--Kris Brice.

"You forgot something, Myth," he says, stepping into
the apartment, brushing fingertips against the softness of my
chin, continuing, "You never came back for your drink at
Studio Dude." In his right hand he holds a bottle of
expensive champagne. Brice passes, heads to the opened
kitchen along the left side of the studio. He finds two glasses,
and begins to open up the champagne as he leans into the
counter, smiling at me.

I've died and gone to Guy-Heaven! Adorable,
twenty-three year old Kris Brice is here in my studio! This
can't be happening. This isn't for real. "How did you find
me, Kris?"

"There's not many people with the name Bernard
Mythington in this city. It wasn't that hard."

I pace around him, to and fro, ask, "Let me
comprehend this. You try picking me up at a local club and I

run out on you, and a few days pass and you show up in my apartment, still wanting to share a drink with me?"

Brice pops the champagne, pours the bubbly liquid, and says, "You're far too cute to stay hidden."

"But I left you, Kris."

He shakes his head, "And I found you. It doesn't matter about the other night. I talked to the bartender and he told me about your friend Spider."

The space between us abruptly closes. Kris Brice moves towards me, wraps one hand around my back, places the other on my hip. "Are you denying me a drink with you, Myth?"

I want to answer him, but again he doesn't give me a chance. His mouth tightens over mine as he rolls his right palm up and down on my back. The kiss is diligent and warm, heavenlike and Prince-worthy. I fall a little against him, losing my balance, feeling heavy and awkward, lumpish. He never does hand me the glass of champagne, does he? Kris Brice embraces me hard with his lean muscles, pulls me up and against him, whispers casually, "You're falling for me, aren't you?"

I don't know what's happening to me. He's famous. I'm a nobody. "I don't know what's going on," I answer.

Brice has everything under control, though. He says he's missed me, nipping at my neck with his lips, pulling off my shirt. "I can't get you out of my mind, Myth." The shirt is tossed to the kitchen's Spanish tile. Brice licks my chest, each nipple, the line of golden hair that drags into my crotch. He lifts off for air, whispers, "It's so nice to see you."

This isn't in any of Prince Charming manuals. Kris has rescued me from my own kitchen, kissing me hard and harder against my chest, slowly biting my shoulders, breathing heavily, rolling hands up and down my back, whispering things to me that I can't possibly begin to comprehend. He's going too fast for me, but I like it, completely become compelled by him, hard for him, seven inches of soft meat growing into eight inches, nine inches ...

I'm sealed to him, cocks meeting and kissing, tongues entwined. It's breathtaking and opulent. I breathe once and only once, take advantage of the second and peel his shirt off and stare at his firm nipples and rigid chest, his biceps and thick wrists. I toss his black shirt to the floor with mine, and say, "That's better, Brice." We continue to kiss until we are drained, until Brice finds the champagne bottle on the kitchen counter, wills me nicely to my knees, and prompts me to arch my back. He pours the soothing and warm liquid down along the plane of my hard and pumped chest, laps it up with greed, and gently cups my package as if we are experienced lovers for the past ten years, meant to be.

I'm his new find, not a toy, but a future character in one of his novels: the man who almost got away. I take his passionate kissing in, allow Kris to use his pointed tongue on each nipple, lapping up the heated liquid, a shared drink between us. His fingers are meticulous as he undoes my leather belt, unbuttons my jeans, and eventually confesses into my ear, "I don't usually do this on a first date, Myth ... but when it comes to you, I can't help myself," as he gently rolls fingers around my veined and throbbing tube of nine inches.

I'm completely naked as he slips out of his jeans, kneels down in front of me and covets the goods between my lightly perspiring legs. I take the euphoric emotion of his mouth over staff in, begin to breathe rapidly and uncontrollably. Kris's head bobs up and down in a rhythmic manner, pulling lips against cock-skin, tasting pre-jizm and evening man in his mouth. He's not an amateur, by far. Kris understands sexual pleasure and satisfaction between two men. Slowly he pulls off, stares up into my brown eyes, and chants, "I want you to lay down, Myth. I've got something to give you."

I listen to him, trusting him, finding him safe and handsome and erotically cleansing. And here on the kitchen floor man lays next to man, stomach to stomach, bodies entwined, with a half-full bottle of champagne nearby. Heads linger between legs in a sixty-nine position as tongues lap majestically and wildly at mushroom-shaped cockheads, carrying out oral relief. We choke together, because our cocks are the same size, because we are perhaps too excited about this moment when man swallows man whole, finding breath and Heaven at the same time, both being nothing less than studio dudes.

Each of us are about to come simultaneously, but it's Brice who pulls away, simply states, "Stand up and hang onto the counter, Myth ... I've been thinking about this moment for days now."

He finds a foil package in his left-behind jeans, rips the square open, and slips the rubber onto his steaming, nine inches of throbbing red spike. Brice coaches, "I'm new to this club, will you show me a good time, dude?"

I'm about to answer him, but there's no time. Inch after inch of his slippery, pushing, penetrating, sliding, slithery writer's meat enters me, causing the room to spin around and around like busy bartenders. Club music vibrates within my ears as my body trembles to Brice's man-tapping. We are like go-go dancers that twist and fly about as the writer and his find whirl in rambunctious and deliberate circles of gay-lust. Six inches turn into seven, seven turn into eight, dividing me, pulverizing my ass, concocting some kind of homo-fire between my kidneys that is purely fantastic. Kris Brice pounds everything into me, spreading me wide and wider, slapping one palm to my ass, creating our own private and personalized club, calling me playful and amative names: *needed boy; sex-magnet; queerfind.*

"More," I whisper loudly, because I want him, because he's famous and all mine, right now. "More, Brice ... More! Drink it up, Brice!" I groan wildly as he pumps and grinds his nine inches into my unyielding space, slapping me on my right ass-cheek again and again, snatching me from reality into faggotdom. The poundage of his swelled and working erection digests my insides continuously, banging me hard and sweetly. We are guy-chimes that twist and ding together, grunting like surprised virgins, moving with passion and grace, needing each other for a bursting end to our sexual closeness. Minute after minute of dude-joy continues. Our hips rock to and fro as my fingers slip against Formica countertop and his heels resume planted into Spanish tile. It is the work of cock inside chute, digging and digging, burning and drilling--Kris Brice finding my soul and our destiny ... together!

It's almost over; I wish it would never end. I hear Brice from behind me groan implicitly, "I'm going to shoot, Myth."

I quickly spin around after he pulls out of me. Quickly, he tosses the condom to the kitchen floor. His slippery abs are covered in man-sweat and the massive pole between his legs. Kris begins to pump the stake with a fervent speed, jacking its skin up and down, holding his breath while doing so.

I savagely follow his movement, thrusting right palm up and down on hardened post. Our eyes lock and we smile at each other, new boyfriends at work, connecting again. It's Kris who says, "I've brought you a present this evening."

"For me?" I ask, dazzled by him, breathing roughly, barely able to answer him, rocking my world as he goes to town on his own meat, pushing hand over stiff mast, bolting hips forward, still smiling.

"Only for you, studio dude," he answers, shooting his load all over my chest, lower neck, and between my legs, dotting my skin with white, sticky bubbles that magically explode against my burning skin.

I'm only seconds behind him in prompting my load to burst forth, decorating his own flesh, piercing his nipples and abs, his biceps and cheeks with my gooey load, flushing my spike up and down with both hands, having my chest constrict wildly. I wash him down in the studio's kitchen with sticky, needy blow, smiling the entire time, and thinking: *When the right guy comes along, it will happen on its own.*

JUMP-BUDDY

~ ~ ~

I was tucked inside one of Corey Drop's huge arms. He was an American dude with massive biceps and a strong hold, just twenty-three years old, but very experienced in jumping. I took a deep breath in … exhaled, and said, "I'm not ready for this."

"I've got you, Keep … You're safe with me." He was the perfect friend who suggested jumping together in the first place; the hottest friend with a terribly delicious looking body that was compiled of steeping sweat, hard nipples, muffed ash colored hair, amethyst-tinted eyes, and a hard nine-incher that—a perfect male-package—pressed into my behind. He yelled over the hum of the plane's engine and my right shoulder, "Ready or not, Keep, here we go!"

I wanted to respond that I wasn't ready, that I was afraid of heights, that I was … *into him* but not the idea of jumping. We were in the lightweight Adelphia 27 plane over Kansas. The jumping door was wide open and wind blew against our bodies. We wore Kennington goggles over our eyes, firm straps around our thick thighs and pumped arms.

95

Tight harnesses were secured over our nicely sculpted torsos and attached in the middle by steel loops and a single pulley. Behind me, on Drop's back was a pack stuffed with a Velocite parachute. We were ready to jump at any second from the Adelphia, which left me nervous and unraveled. It was my first jump, and I felt that it was the last day of my homo-life. It was crazy … it was unreal.

"This is a total turn on for me, you know that?"

I felt his hard cock of propeller against my ass as he stood behind me.

"Yeah," I quivered, scared out my mind, lying.

Over the plane's humming engine, he confided, "There's nothing to be afraid of, Keep. I'm here for you. Drop has you."

"It's a high jump, though."

"It's only two thousand feet. I've got you, buddy. You're not going anywhere. Be brave and do it with me."

I was strapped to his stomach, facing away from him, looking down into blue-green nothingness. I wanted to be grounded and able to breathe right again. I wanted nothing to do with the jump, the Adelphia, or Kansas.

Behind me, Drop ground his cock into my ass again, in an unexpected manner of desire. He laughed out loud with an adrenaline rush. And then—suddenly, unexpectedly, shockingly—I felt his narrow lips against the back of my neck, his tongue against my skin, and his hand firmly pressed around my body as fingers gently groped my Hardington suit, covering my crotch with his right palm. Drop rubbed his fingers into my beam, caused it to grow somewhat hard. He was touching me for the very first time, catching me off guard, making me crazy, prompting a questionable tingle to *jump* through my body. The kiss felt warm and tender, quick and everlasting. His tongue was slippery and just right with its long strokes. And as his airborne tenderness was carefully executed, instantly he pushed us out into the wild blue yonder over Kansas, yelling at the top of his lungs, "Time to jump!"

Before I knew it, we were falling into that space between heaven and earth ...

Falling. Falling. Falling. We zoomed through that empty void, heading towards the Kansas earth. I screamed at the top of my lungs as Drop laughed heartily behind me. I was elated and high, unable to breathe, possibly hyperventilating. Behind me, Drop was fully into the spirit of jumping too, was completely hard against my ass, screaming at the top of his lungs with pleasure.

At about twelve-hundred feet he pulled a cord and there was red, white, and blue smoke that whizzed out of the bottom of his pack, streamed behind us like a kite's string or a puppy dog's tail. We flew left and right, zigzagged through the blue-blue sky. I felt poetic and safe against him, sinfully overjoyed, was hard between my legs, and ready to blow a load into mid-day. I was beyond thrilled and ready to cream the inside of the Hardington suit, was over-excited and feeling the charge of a lifetime. The drop was gratifying and dick-jolting, mind-blowing and vigorous—a rush with Drop that would be the first of many to come.

As we hit the ground with ease he unclipped a strap on his harness and the parachute was let free. We landed safely, rolled over a few times on Kansas's good earth. And once completely grounded, my world spinning around and around, my nine inches of steeping hot shaft ready to burst with country-sap, Drop unharnessed his pack from his back and unbuckled me from his chest. My bud crawled around me on his hands and knees, faced me, laid me on my back, and smiled down at me, "You okay, pal?"

I shook my head in a contemptible manner and smiled back up at him. "That was the fucking most insane thing I've ever done. I'm okay, though." He leaned over my chest, pressed a palm along my sweaty forehead and through my hair in a somewhat discreet manner, accidentally had his suit-covered rod press against my own privates and said, "Davey Keep, you're one hell of a jumper."

I sat up and against him, had my chest against Drop's chest, breathed his heavy and musky aroma in, choked on my own excitement, and responded, "You win the bet, I guess."

"I do, don't I?"

"I said if you got me to jump I was to owe you something tender and delicious. Dinner, I guess. Like a char-broiled steak, right?"

There wasn't anyone around except for the pilot in the Adelphia, and Cutter was already heading back to the airstrip, three miles away. Our eyes connected. He breathed into me, over me, consumed my aroma, looked bedazzled and sweetly mellow. Corey Drop said, "I was thinking about something else, Davey."

"Like what?"

Then—suddenly, unexpectedly, shockingly—he cupped his right hand to my chin, faced me with a constant, amethyst stare, leaned down and over me, brought his lips to my thinly-lined mouth that had just turned twenty-one, and kissed me hard, like no other guy before.

I melted beneath him in the field. I felt dizzy and confused, was believing I was still dropping out of the sky. The sliver of his tongue scurried back the necessary shaft of my throat, played with my own tongue, and kept wildly busy. I felt his cupped palm on my burning crotch, toying with me, playing with me, prompting a buzzing feeling to stir within my mind, and allowing me grow harder than hard.

Eventually he pulled off and away, was sweaty and huffing. Drop said, "That's what I wanted. Something tender and delicious."

I laughed at him, thought him straight and into girls, said rather quietly, "How long have you wanted to do that?"

He shrugged his shoulders, "A while."

"You ever do that with a guy before?"

Drop shook his head. "Never really wanted to, Keep. Just you."

"Just me?"

"The one and only."

His VR-2000 walkie talkie against his right hip chirped, interfering with our moment. It was Cutter's scratchy voice asking, "You dudes okay down there? … Over."

Drop pulled away from my shivering body, sat up, peered down at me with a broaching smile, and said into the handset, "Everything's looking better than great here, Cutter. We're going to get something to eat. Thanks for the drop … Over."

"Don't have too much fun without me," Cutter warned, "Over."

"I'm losing you, Cutter … Over," and Drop flicked the OFF button on his handset, which left us to nothing more than the heated sun, a Kansas field, and his first boyfriend—me!

His S-10 pick-up was parked in the shade on his daddy's property. I recall how Drop slipped the parachute behind the front seat of the truck, turned to me and said, "I've been wanting to tell you something, Keep." He pulled out a bag of sorts, unzipped it and left the canvas flap open; I saw clothes inside for him to change into.

"What do you want to tell me?"

Drop, to my surprise unzipped his Hardington suit to his mid-section. Hypnotically I peered at rock-hard abs and a chest of steel. One of his pointed nipples was visible and I licked my lips with generous craving as it was sweaty and firm. Beneath his naval was a trail of thick dark hair that sported a triangular patch of pubes. Drop saw my unintentional interest and said, "It's kind of a secret."

"I'm good for secrets," I confessed.

"It's something you're not going to expect."

I replied civilly, "You're my jump-buddy. I'm ready for anything."

"It's about *us*."

I knew that, honestly. Because he was nervous, and because I wanted to help him and make his coming out easy, I pointed to his goods and uttered with a smile, "That's not so bad to show off, you know."

Drop laughed in a husky and masculine manner and responded, "Since you're looking, you might as well see the whole thing. Do you have any complaints about that?"

Before I could respond he was already stepping out of his jumpsuit. Drop smiled at me and I smiled back. My eyes shifted down the length of his solidly ripped body, a half-hard jet poking out of his middle. He asked quite proudly, "What do you think, Keep? You like what you see?"

I rubbed saliva away from my bottom lip, blinked once, began to feel eight inches of shaft bob up and down in my suit. I replied in a man-spell, "Nice piece, Drop. My question is simple, though … Do you know how to use it?"

Drop—with two palms and pulsating smile—reached down between his legs, man-handled his beef, and uttered seductively, "I think you're the man to tell me that, Keep. Now show me what you have."

He was impressed with my solid eight inches of gear, couldn't keep his lips off the condom-covered rod. Drop was new at blow-jobs, but I wasn't complaining. As I stood over him and held his sweaty-slick shoulders, warm salvia smeared over his face as he tried to suck all eight inches of my rod the entire way down and into his tight, virgin throat. Occasionally, he choked and gagged, backed off, found field air, and then continued. He rubbed his muscular hands up and down the plane of my chest as I leaned into his truck, yanked on my nipples, played with my firm abs, groaned and moaned beneath me with utter man-bliss.

Still hungry, he pulled away and said, "You're too hot for me."

"How long have you been into me, Drop?"

"Doesn't matter, does it? … I like you, that's all that matters."

Once again, I was tucked inside one of Corey Drop's huge arms. We kissed like real men in the shade of the oak tree and eventually I coached him through fore-play, told him that I had a surprise for him, " ... something you've never felt before," and spun his naked body around on the tailgate, bucked his legs apart, slipping plastic over my tongue.

And in that field of gold, summer bursting around us, he yelled out my name with euphoria as his homo-hidden mind spun around and around with the pressure of my fingers prying his unused ass open. My tongue dove into his tight hole, pleasuring him, causing him to feel lighter and all mine, for the first time; the perfect couple—us. I licked his hole repeatedly, hungrily, again and again, until he complained about shooting his load too soon, until his rod bounced between his hard legs, desiring nothing less than my wholesome ass and guy-chute for his pumping delight.

He suggested in front of me, "I want to do something I've never done before to a guy, Keep ... are you game?"

I stood and faced Drop and smiled at him as I brushed ash colored hair away from his amethyst colored eyes. Our sweaty chests stuck together with a stinging closeness. I felt his rod pressed against my rod, and in time pulled away from his mouth, saying what he had chanted to me about a half hour before, "I've got you, Drop ... You're safe with me."

Drop laughed and added, "I thought you'd say that."

I found another condom in the cab of the truck and slipped it over his nine inch pole as he stood beside me. Before spinning around and placing my hands on the tailgate, spreading my legs and opening up my soul for Corey Drop, I kissed him hard on the lips, pulled away, and said, "Ready or not, here we go."

I gasped wildly upon his immediate entrance. He thrust two quick inches into me and pulled out, teasing me. Drop hung onto my hips, pushed into me again, playing with me. I called out in splendid pain in front of him, felt four inches separate me, then five … six … and seven. In back of me, solidly still inside my ass, I listened to him supply, "Two more inches to go, Keep. No harm … no foul."

Before I knew it the two final inches of his pole was driving its way into my asshole, breaking me apart. Drop knew what to do, of course. He bolted inside me, pulled out, ripped into me again, nine inches of steeping shaft pivoting in me with dexterity and stiff performance. Drop held me tight as if we were jumping together again, riding me from behind, socking his cock deeply inside me, pulling out of me, and saying rather greedily, "I'm here for you. Drop has you."

We were wild and rhythmical together as man pumped inside man, as he held me towards him, one hand firmly wrapped around my stomach as his other hand toyed with my balls between my legs. I was his jump-buddy and he wasn't going to stop until our flight ended. He rammed everything into me, played with the hard stem between my legs, kissed my back with his opened mouth, and enjoyed our moment together as if we were nothing more than two jumpers gliding down and through the Kansas sky, plummeting to earth with grace and beauty.

I screamed at the top of my lungs as Drop laughed heartily behind me, pumping me in his rowdy manner. I was elated and high, unable to breathe, possibly hyperventilating. Behind me, Drop was fully into the spirit of things, was completely hard, screaming at the top of his lungs too, with pleasure. Together we breathed like wild men, sweaty and untamed, prosaically moving with a swiftness that was rich and filled masculine beauty until he said, "I want to shoot now, Keep."

I couldn't answer him because there wasn't enough time. He quickly pulled out of me and carefully spun me around. I saw him rip off the condom and toss it into the back of the truck. He began to work his meat up and down with both hands, facing me. Muscles in his neck vibrated as fingers worked protein. His entire body was sweaty and all hard, ready to pop his load onto the Kansas earth.

"It's coming," he informed.

"I'm ready to jump," I chanted back. I was toying with my own goods and not even realizing it, ready to come at any second. My own appendages worked cock in a fastidious manner.

"It's— " he couldn't finish his sentence. The dude was ready to drop his load everywhere. One second he was bolting his hips forward and having his hands move in a brisk manner up and down on his pole. The next moment, he was firing his load toward the ground, decorating the golden grass with globs of white sap, breathing heavily and uncontrollably, shooting and shooting juice from his jumper, until he was spent.

"You can do it, Keep," he coached.

I bolted my hips forward, was holding my spike with an uncontainable spirit, and eventually fired off my own load into the grassy spot where we stood. In doing so, I called out his name over and over, bucked my hips wildly, sprayed creamy goo everywhere, until there was nothing more in my man-spigot to shoot.

Afterwards, both of us breathing heavily in the Kansas heat, I held him to me and hugged him hard, pressed my chest into his. I kissed his neck and listened to him ask, "How long have you known about my secret?"

"Not long … maybe a week ago … maybe today."

"Can I keep you?" he asked sweetly.

I pulled away from him, connected my eyes with Drop's. "It's all in the name, isn't it?" I asked, grasped him towards me, and kissed him the way he wanted a jump-buddy like me to kiss.

MAN-FIND

~ ~ ~

We were post-sexed and breathing heavily, both of us tucked inside the city apartment and out of the springtime rain. Overtop me, I felt my boyfriend's naked and chiseled body stick to my own. I liked to talk after our intimate moments; Van Harden didn't. Huffing for air and craving a cigarette, I dreamily glanced into the electrician's aqua colored eyes and said, "It's not kinky, Van, it's just different."

The sculpted boy-doll with the broad shoulders and massive pecs was still hard between his legs, compressed to my body. "I don't know if I can do it again."

"Of course, you can. Anyway, how much do you like me?"

He dove his tongue inside my mouth, smelling of my own sweat and spent liquids. I felt his hard poker against my ab-lined stomach. He pulled out of my mouth, kept the back of my hands pressed to the sheets with his boyfriend-palms and caused my stiff prick to vibrate between my legs again, ready for a second round—any time ... any place. Van came off for air and said, "Too much, Pack."

I giggled beneath him, rolled a hand down the plane of his muscled back and responded, "Then you'll do it, right?"

He kept licking the cords on my neck, rolling his tongue down and over the meat, completely and wholesomely enchanted with his find. Van came up for air a second time and said, "Blonde or brown hair this time?"

I wanted to spray a creamy load from my rod again as he rolled his firm protein into my abs. Instead, I prevented the mess and whispered, "I was thinking completely bald this time. Shocking hazel eyes. Someone with a tight ass for me to fuck."

"A jock?" He rolled fingers over my skin, prosaically, mechanically and stupendously. Man over man, driving me wild.

I shook my head, trying to hold back a second load from shooting everywhere. "No, not a jock. I want a white collar man this time."

"An intern?"

"No, not an intern. Someone around our age … twenty-five or –six. An experienced man."

"An executive, Pack?"

He sat up, lapping sticky goo up from my chest. Sweetly, I breathed underneath him, toying with his hard nipples, "Now you're catching on."

He longed to be done again and again, and again, continuously, rapturously, following through with our afternoon game that we had called Spring Heat. He pulled off me, rolled onto the sticky sheets and smiled at me, "Where can I find this guy?"

Had I fallen for Van? I think. I couldn't help it and rolled fingers through his cocoa colored hair, whispering to him, "I know the perfect place … It's not far from here. We can shower together, and afterwards, I'll take you there."

It was springtime and the need to find someone we could share was relevant. Our annual event of seeking out the right guy and sharing an intimate moment with him, longingly kept me active. Our pursuit was almost over, though, and I couldn't dream of not obeying our spring hungers, fulfilling our desires to the fullest.

I pressed a white shirt for Van, popped his tight ass into a pair of dress pants and Italian shoes, sprayed him with Intense, decorated him with a silk tie that showed off the humps of his massive chest, called him, "Yummy, just right, and ready to go."

"Where?"

"Emeril's Lounge."

"We're not members." He looked deliciously perfect in the get-up. Out of his realm, but chiseled with all the right clothes and accessories.

I clung to his brawn, kissed his neck, and whispered into his ear, "Trust me, Van, we don't have to be members to get into Emeril's Lounge. You're so hot right now, any high-end place would have you. Believe me, you're going to have fun this evening."

Emeril's Lounge. The place was top crust. The place was like walking onto the set of *Law & Order*: professionally upbeat, stringent and powerful. It was a playground for elite men. A cigar bar where straight men could get away from their wives or girlfriends. A place I had been eyeing up for weeks, needing to peruse, admire, and taste.

Van had an imported beer and I chose a dry martini. Van asked, "Do you see anything you like?"

"Besides you?"

"That was nice," he whispered. "Anyone but me?"

I peered around the lounge while drinking the rather strong drink. Aristocratic lawyers, accountants, doctors and high-end executives were in packs, all of which were smoking and drinking. A live jazz band played in the corner. Young boys with cute eyes and unpounded asses waited tables in penguin suits. I studied everyone in the lounge, breathed in and out, finished off my martini and said, "Right over there, do you see him?"

Van did. The guy was a model. Hairless with green eyes. Broad shoulders like Van, slim body with just enough muscle to hang onto. Slender cheeks and a corded neck. Bright red lips. A minutely lined scar on his upper lip; an accident from his boyhood. A nice find for the evening. Ours to share and take back to the apartment if we wanted him badly enough. "Nice," Van said. "Real nice. He has a rough and sexy look about him with just enough zest."

I chuckled heartily at that, numb with passion, lust, a semi-erection with thoughts of the hairless gentlemen getting it on with my boyfriend in our shared bed.

The guy caught Van and me looking at him, which prompted us to steer our views elsewhere. Van said, "He spotted us. Besides, he's out of our league."

"You like me, right?" I asked Van.

He sighed heavily, contentedly, like putty in my hands. "I do."

"Then do your thing. I'll be back in the apartment waiting for the both of you."

"What if I can't?" sweet Van asked.

"You will," I replied, placed my empty martini glass on the table and walked out.

We've done this twice before. The first, with a blue collar electrician, one of Van's coworkers that I couldn't prevent myself from holding his hips and pumping everything I had into his tight asshole. The second time was with a football jock, a sophomore from Templeton College. It was a game Van and I had both enjoyed, a willful act between men that we agreed upon. We forced no one to have sex with us. We were not cruel or vicious. We weren't in love with our visitors. Together, we desired nothing less than their rippled skin and pulsating flesh, their hard bodies and shafts, their succulent lips against our own chests or thighs—anywhere. We were not animals, mind you. We desired a chosen man who was a consensual adult. A man with needs. A person whom knew in advanced—even before stepping into the apartment—what would fully occur between three young men, together, as one.

It was a high. It was delectable. It was the epitome of homo-eroticism. It was our lives and we were enjoying it to the fullest.

I decided the living room would work. I lighted candles and poured three glasses of wine. I showered, again, and freshly shaved, and eventually slipped into a silk robe the color of the hairless man's lips. I put on jazz music to remind our guest of Emeril's Lounge. I filled a bowl with unopened condoms and placed them next to the couch, tubes of lubrications and creams, too. I found warm chocolate, strawberries and freshly whipped cream, in case our guest was hungry. I had prepared well, ready.

They arrived on time, just before ten o'clock. Van introduced our guest to me by using only his first name, "This is Erich." A nice name for a very nice looking man.

"It's a pleasure to meet you, Erich." He smiled at me, seeming shy and tender, absolutely perfect and flawless for my needs. "You look as if you need a drink to take the edge off."

Erich nodded his head, as expected, and for the next half hour or so we drank wine together, nibbled on chocolate-dipped strawberries, listening to the jazz. We danced together, just the three of us. We kissed like men, pressing our tongues into each others' mouths, down along necks and over chins. I tasted both Van and Erich, enjoying their flesh, desiring them to kiss me back, toying with my bliss.

I was pressed between a clothed Van and Erich. I turned my head towards Erich's ear and whispered, "Please don't be afraid. We're very safe. We won't hurt you. We are honest but sexual men."

"I'm not afraid," the accountant whispered back, diving his tongue into the farthest reaches of my mouth, kissing me hard and harder.

I pulled away and watched my handsome Van kiss Erich's scar above his red lips, his forehead and then his right cheek. I listened to Van whisper, "Can I undress you, Erich?"

"Yes," Erich responded, standing still and stern, unmoving and ready for whatever was about to come next, taken and charmed by our springtime playfulness.

Erich's chest was a block of abs, sculpted to perfection. His nipples were hard and pointed. I watched Van kiss the nipples, once, twice, three times. I gazed at Van's tongue as it worked diligently over the accountant's skin, thirsty for the guest's perspiration. The stranger was *completely* hairless and freshly shaven. His golden skin glimmered in the candle's flickering light as Van continuously and sweetly kissed the gentleman's biceps, his armpits, the lines in his neck and along the plain of his chest.

We didn't ask him to slip out of his pants; Erich accomplished this act on his free will. He dropped the pants by the couch and showed off his cleanly shaven balls and uncut, erect cock that was ten inches long and two inches thick—a perfect subject in a world full desirable men.

"Would you like to see what you've gotten yourself into?" I asked Erich, referring to what was hidden under my robe.

"Yes," he replied softly, ready for anything. "Please."

As my dark-haired Van stood beside me and stripped out of his suit and pants, a full erection bouncing between his stern and pumped looking legs, I dropped my robe for both to view my perfect body.

Immediately, Erich smiled and said, "Nine inches ... I like that."

"Right you are, my friend. Wait until you feel it inside you."

Van, while generously stroking his steeping tool, politely asked our guest to find his way down to the floor and kindly get on all fours.

I winked and smiled at Van, kissing him hard, dragging my lips across his, touching his chest with my skin, adoring his comment, placing dibs on the man's mouth to covet my cock while Van was busy behind him.

Before positioning ourselves in a stately manner around the accountant from Emeril's Lounge, I looked down at our prey on his hands and needs, civil and ready for our meaty combination. Van—a divine and ripped saint who was charged with nothing less than boyish charm—moved up and behind our gentleman friend and positioned himself on his knees. Politely Van spread the guest's buttocks open with two fingers, admired his discovery and waited for me to stand on the opposite side of the accountant.

The accountant—an erotic species who should have been in the pages of *Men's Fitness*—was not squeamish or timid, was perhaps eager to assist our personal needs, explained rather jovially, "I'm ready when you guys are you. Don't let me down."

Together, like heated lovers who are committed to each other until the end of time, we blissfully labored over Erich. Handling my pulsating cock, I prompted its mass into his open mouth, slipping into his saliva-hole quickly and wildly, gagging him in a generous but harmless manner. And Van, my boyfriend, the guy who really liked me enough to find that pleasure between us, positioned his tongue against the accountant's pink hole, lapping at it contentedly, prosaically, and masterfully.

There was groaning and moaning. As I bolted my cumbersome nine inches of prick into the guest's mouth I watched our guest arch his back to the splendorous tongue-massage that Van was sharing with him. I called over the young man's firm back, "Are you enjoying yourself, Van?"

Van slurped ass juices, pulled off, smiled up at me with tight rump in his face, and said in a chipper manner, "I think we've found ourselves a keeper, Benjamin."

I giggled with contentment, gagging the accounting and calling back down to Van, "He needs broken in a little bit more and then he'll be just fine."

Erich, between us, hunched over and balancing himself on his hands and knees, was beautiful in action. He was sweaty and graceful, perfect for our needs. As Van opened up the hairless man's sliver with a protected tongue, Erich gnawed vigorously on my cock, hungrily, leaving me numb with passion, delirious and pleased above him. At one point, I almost lost my balance. Immediately I clung my palms to the guest's sweaty shoulders and breathed healthily in on the pungent man-air wafting about the room. I listened to the jazz and Erich's groaning. The smell of strong and concentrated sex spun magically around the three of us. The aroma of man-need. The obsession and permissible enthusiasm of men who were connected.

He would come if we didn't stop; I knew that for a fact. Erich was a strong man but if we hadn't pulled out of him, if we hadn't thought of his emotions and his physical will, he would have spewed everywhere, without even touching himself. As I released my cock from his mouth, I kindly said to Van, "Are you ready for something different?"

Van pulled away from the piece of ass, breathed heavily in and out, seemed awestruck and mesmerized with the event at hand, answering me in a quite satisfied tone, "Yes ... please."

I don't know what came over me. I don't know why I was so attracted sexually to Erich. As he stood and faced me, a pre-bubble of goo leaking out of his man-joint, I found myself kissing him on the lips and closing my eyes. I touched the ten inches of pick between his legs, breathed him into my soul, adored his skin as it was pressed against mine, and eventually pulled away. I was moved by him. Taken. Trapped. Needing him in a different manner. No longer did

I want to pound his smooth and hairless ass. No longer did I want to place my hands on his hips and thrust my pole into his masculine core. No longer did I want to—

"He wants to fuck you," Van whispered, "I can see it in his eyes."

"Yes," I whispered, "I think he does."

"Of course," Erich whispered., "but only if Van kindly gets in on the action."

It was agreed among the three of us. Sex among men. Heated and lust-driven pleasure for each of us. An agreement. Consensual, again. Men at play. It was time.

He wanted and desired us more than we him. Erich applied a condom to his ten inches and told me to lay down on the floor, which I did. And after spreading my legs, wide and wider, a pink hole for him to tease and probe, for his hot spike to gently roll in and out of, he nicely asked Van to step in front of him so he could mouth his rod.

It was poetry in motion: the instructor, the electrician and the guest. As Erich teased my nipples with fingertips, I felt four inches of his rocket slip into my soul, then a fifth, a sixth, and he eventually pulled out. I watched him lap at my boyfriend's cock, taking all of the eight inches into the back of his throat and pulling away. Off and on. Off and on. Rapturous beauty that was glorious between them, rocking into each other, moving together and in docile manners.

All of Erich's steeping, bulging and erect mass entered my core with one blow, pulsating within me, causing me to feel dreamy and relaxed, numb with delight beneath his weight. His motion was rhythmic and complacent to my desires, and I instructed him with a sultry whisper, "Deeper, Erich … Please,"

And he listened to me, pounding my ass full of his rod, breaking me down, building within me, holding my legs apart, causing me to lose my breath and consciousness, tenderly. I felt weakened by his weight, vibrating with him and against him, allowing his stem to comfortably protrude

112

into the farthest reaches of my gaydom, breaking me apart, feeding me inch after inch of wholesome stranger.

Above me, I watched Van glide in and out of Erich's mouth, filling the guest's center with his meat, holding the back of the gentleman's head, enjoying the ride. Van's inner thighs dripped with steamy perspiration on my skin, burning and sizzling my flesh, sinking into my pores as if it were a cure for my man-need. He murmured words I could not understand, a lamenting of sorts that I found exhilarating and stimulating. Man-chanting or man-humming that drove me wild, needing both Van and Erich more.

And sweetly, devouring every moment with that third find who had found it to be a conventional notion to pound my firm ass, I groaned as he thrust all ten inches into my hole, hammering me, riding me, bucking me in a wildly transfixed manner that was heated and just right. I called out both of their names at the top of my lungs as sweat from Van's chest dripped onto my nipples, decorating them, and then I whispered to Erich, "You're what we wanted. You're our find. Please, make it harder."

Van pounded the guest's throat, again and again, continuously. Van was in ecstasy with our keep, working Erich's mouth with skill, plunging his eight inches deeper and deeper into his throat, groaning as he moved, balancing himself above me so he wouldn't fall. A skilled lover at work on what he had brought home. What he had found. Ours for the night.

Ten throbbing and hard inches bucked my opening. Willingly. Sharply. He anesthetized my body with his movements. Erich drove me crazy beneath him, pushing everything into me, holding onto my legs, pounding me dry, causing me to feel lighter and dazed, dizzy and confused, but perfectly rational at the same time.

"He's too much for me." It was Van who was going to come first. Quickly, he pulled himself free from the guest's tight mouth and stood over my body, working his strapping joint between his legs. "He's hotter than I ever anticipated."

Erich, our shaven and hairless discovery, pulled out of me. He gently dropped my legs and stood, ripping the plastic free from his cock and tossing it off to the side. His chest thumped wildly because of his romp, in and out, breathlessly.

Above me they stood kissing with their eyes closed, with their chests almost pressed together, with their perspiration dripping onto my skin, burning me with self-contentment. Their nipples almost touched as they smiled like young and gleeful boys. Grateful for their nicely sculpted bodies, for an evening that could easily be considered safe and extraordinary, I watched them move their hands up and down on their shafts, fists working at full speed, tongues tangled, temporary lovers at work. I studied their movements with accuracy, adoring their efforts, desiring both of them to come on me, shooting their loads onto my skin. Men at work. The accountant and electrician sharing a dance between men. Sexual likenesses found.

I copied their movements, bucking my hips and toying with myself, ready to blast my own shoot against my skin. As I watched them rock steadily above me, I manipulated my rod, playing with it, massaging its veins and length, ready at any second to come with both of them. My breathing increased. I couldn't think. My body was vibrating methodically on the floor in some kind of ultra-sexual convulsion. I couldn't—

It was Erich who pulled out of the kiss. He simply whispered, "Now," and shot his hot spray of ooze against my chest, searing my abs.

"For you," Van answered, looking down at me, firing his load onto my upper chest, burning my shoulders and neck beneath him.

I was last to come. They watched me blast an arc of white, glistening goo up and between their still-stiff cocks. The burst twirled around and flung back down to earth,

114

landing on my chest, mixing with my skin, causing a numbness to form within my body and mind. Droplets of come spotted me with ease, layering my flesh, burning my pores, and leaving me feel desired and needed—between men, between us. A trio of lust.

We were driven and spent, and now our third visitor was consumed. Together, on the floor, we kissed and laughed after clean-up. I held both of them against me, around me, becoming spent with them, exhausted. I whispered to Van, "Thank you, you do like me." And then I turned to Erich—our most favorite, our find and keep—and simply kissed him on his neck, pulled away, and said with a smile, running my hand against his right cheek, "Will you please come again, I'll miss you."

KNOB POLISHING

~ ~ ~

I'm literally swept away by twenty-six year old Tag Alisar, gawk at his chiseled, Latino, and pumped body in the reflective, Louis XIV mirror. He's fixing the sprouts of his Navy-man cut. Tag pushes his dark and sweaty hair back, smiles like a prized and gallant street fighter or superstar model. His faintly colored amethyst eyes catch my view behind him in the mirror's image ... and he smiles a clever, egotistical grin that is drop-dead fascinating. Slowly, with a skill that is intoxicating and stinging, he moves the fingers down along his bulky pecs and nipples. Next, the busy appendages find abs and travel southward-bound, seeking out a seven inch soft package that is secretly hidden behind abraded denim.

"Lift!" he calls out my last name, "Whatcha lookin' at, dude?"

I shake my head, "Nothing, Tag."

"You lying to me, Timmy Lift? ... Cause if you are ..." He turns around instead of finishing his sentence, shows off his delivery to me, knowing completely well that my eyes are glued to nothing less than his stiffening niceness.

He's looking at my piercing and serious brown eyes, at the crop of my blond hair and tiny earlobes, narrow lips, and refined jaw. And maybe, just maybe, Tag likes what he sees, enjoys the visual splendor of a twenty year old crotch and hips and chest and ...

"I'm not lying ... really." I'm slightly intimidated by his bulkiness. The Peruvian god stands over six feet tall and weighs well over two hundred pounds. Tag can kick my ass with a flick of his fingers, or by exhaling a mere breath from his reddish, South American lips. He's rock-hard muscle with attitude, cuts to the chase, and is adorably stimulating.

He jokes with me (dimples shining with new perspiration and naked chest bulging with excessive, dark muscle-meat) as he cups his goods with one large palm. "If you want it, Timmy ... It's all yours."

I resist the emphatic temptation to close the six foot gap between us, bend down on my hurting knees, open my mouth, and merely drag my craving tongue over his precious and hardening goods. Instead, with my heart thumping nervously within my chest, I respond, "We need to get back to work, Tag."

"Yeah, I know. Let's bring the settee in next."

We're in the furniture delivery/moving business. My dad has this company called Lift's Moving. During summer and winter vacations from UCLA, and those occasional long weekends off, I help Tag out, and make a few bucks on the side.

As for Tag Alisar, he's a full-time employee, and has worked for my father for the past eight years. In the evening he's one of those nightclub strippers for the ladies, with very little modesty, flashing smiling, and a dazzling body that brings home the bucks. In all honesty, he's every guy I've ever wanted to slip against, have my chest clamp to, and feel his tongue drive majestically down the sliver of my man-needing throat.

117

It's not possible. It will never be possible. There are two reasons. One, Tag is moving this weekend to Phoenix, Arizona where he wants to buy up property for resale. And two, Tag is into women, not guys, I believe. He's all buffed and hard, perfectly molded with muscles, a rough-riding, Latino cowboy who can't get enough. I don't stand a chance of becoming singular with him; the odds are against me.

We're outside the Wellington Estate in the half-circle drive, south of Beverly Hills. The twenty-four foot moving truck stands open. The winter-warm California, mid-day air grazes my cheeks and shoulders. Tag clamps one of my shoulders with his massive palms, stares at me, and states, "The Wellington's got some nice shit, huh?"

He's the one with the nice shit, and knows it. I say, "Pretty much so. Let's get the settee now."

We climb into the back of the truck together. Tag goes first and I admire his tight ass, stare usefully at the rounded bubbles. Uncontrollably, I lick my lips, readjust my stiffening seven inches of Tag-want, and begin the trek behind him.

There's a problem with my technique, though. As I jump off the ground, fly upwards like Superman, I make the leap into the truck, but my landing is not of a gymnast's eloquence. I'm sloppy and off-kilter, fly towards him, land on my hands and knees, and feel my lips graze his sizable package between V-goodness.

Of course I take a promising whiff of his goods, feel captivated by the strong and masculine aroma that teases my nostrils. And slowly, I pull myself up, clamping hands onto his carved hips, balancing myself, eventually standing.

He has his palms on my sides, keeps me from falling again. Our lips are implicitly close, awarding permission to kiss, but we don't. As our cocks touch and our hips graze ever so slightly against each other's, there is a moment of immediate silence, leaving our eyes to intricately connect: sloppy brown with shimmering amethyst.

He's serious for a change; it relaxes me. "You have something on your cheek, Timmy."

"I do?"

"Grease or something … maybe furniture polish." Tag—with a steadiness that is impeccable—draws a finger to my cheek, and pulls the smear of grease away. "I got it."

"You sure?"

"Yes." His dim-purple eyes tell a story that is contrary to the rumors floating about the company. I see that he's comfortable against me, reflects no embarrassment or remorse with our brief connection. Tag Alisar is perfectly at ease with my lower torso caressing his English cock introducing itself to Latino cock, forming a mixed ratio of question.

I am overwhelmed that he doesn't push me away and into the Elizabethan, quatersawn oak settee, or Chippendale desk with claw feet and cabriole legs. To my utter and shaft-raising surprise, Tag leans into my ear, capsizes my head to his hulking chest, and whispers in the most Knight in Shining Armor manner, "What's a guy to do with a hot number like you in his arms?"

I can't take it. Every ounce of energy seems to pound in the tippy-top portion of my cock's head. Unexplainable vibrations taunt my mind and cause me to feel light-headed. I promptly slip down from his arms and drag my body along his. A cheek meets pointed and hard nipple, rounded ab, and a somewhat hardening package with massive, left thigh nearby. I unintentionally wilt to the bed of the truck and feel my eyes completely close. There is nothing more and nothing less than an abyss of pure blackness—I faint and become lost.

Eventually I come to and Tag whispers into my ear, "You're okay now … I'm right here."

"What happened?" I groggily question.

He has me cupped into his cradling arms. "You fainted."

"Fainted? I've never fainted in my entire life."

Tag chuckles next to me, "There's a first time for everything, isn't there, Timmy?"

"What else happened, Tag?" I want to hear about our bodies together, about how he kissed me to wake me up, about that mere moment in the windblown afternoon that allowed a Latino stripper to become captivated by another guy.

Tag Alisar responds nervously, shaking his head, "Nothing."

"Of course."

And as he allows me to sit up on my own, our moment of lust, needs, and togetherness is easily and sinfully abandoned.

We unload the truck like good workers. All of the Wellington's furniture is placed into the house exactly where they desire it. We're on the second floor of the Victorian mansion in Mrs. Wellington's bedroom, polishing the knobs on a Louis XVI chest of drawers that collects dust during the move. The brown polish in our sixteen ounce tub is low, and Tag professionally informs me, "We need more goop, guy."

"I'll run down to the truck and get a new tub."

"Sounds good. I'll be waiting for you."

I'm gone for about two minutes, tops. When I return with the new plastic tub of Briwax furniture polish, I stand a foot inside Mrs. Wellington's exquisite bedroom and utter in a rather stunned demeanor, "What the hell?"

It's Tag who floors me. Alisar stands next to the sleigh bed with his worn jeans pushed down to his ankles. His legs are spread apart and I see that he sports a Latino-steel pole just for me. As the pounder grows hard and harder on his body, he smiles at me, toying with my emotions. Tag chants, "I'm just showing you an extra piece of furniture that needs some polishing, dude?"

He's fucking with me again, playing a queer game, leaving me feel tense and teased by the harassing meat that pivots from his elaborately muscled body. I won't fall for it, though, and begin to shake my head. "Put the package away, Tag ... we've got work to do."

He doesn't listen to me, answers, "Damn right, we do." Alisar moves a steady hand down the plane of his rugged chest, over the line of dark treasure-trail hair that leads into the triangle of pubes, spins it palm-up, spits into it, and rolls it down and over his erect staff, beginning to manipulate it with a saliva-moistened grip.

It's an action that I find remotely dick-vibrating. I can't help from staring at Tag with his hand-working-cock motion. My own piece of wood spurts to life, and becomes challenged by the heated moment to retain dormant.

With his free hand, Tag catches a long, white and sticky looking strand of pre-guy-ooze in an available and cupped palm. He moves the palm up to his mouth and devours the afternoon man-snack, causing me to spurt a few drops of my own salty jizm into tightening jeans.

As he maneuvers his hand over his Peruvian joint, Tag says, "Do you know what I want, Timmy?"

I am still stunned, now impressively hard. Yet stupidly, I shake my head, and say, "I'm not sure, Tag."

He's dexterous with his free hand, uses his pointing finger as an instrument to draw me towards him, and adds, "I want to polish your knob, dude ... Stop being so shy."

"Knob? ... Mine?"

"Yes, yours. Now get your cock out and bring it over here before I blast a load."

Tag Alisar is out of his beloved, south of the border mind. I don't believe him for a second that he wants to gnaw on my grade-A beef. He's setting me up for a bad joke, for humiliation and—

I move up to him anyway, recollect his Prince Charming lips against my own when he generously awakened me from blackness. If he's not joshing me, and honestly craves me, then he'll suck on my rod like a good Latino stripper. But if he's not, then I deserve what's coming, a mere overdose of gay foolishness. I take the chance, though, and slowly move forward, step by step, until I reach him.

And once in his confines, standing in front of him, with Tag's lips pressed against mine, the post-flavor of spew still on his mouth, he kisses me hard, digging his tongue between my teeth. Tag unzips my zipper, frees my unyielding extension from jeans (no underwear, of course), and presses my cock against the naked length of his own in a heated, frenzied rod-dance.

He's not kidding me. His sexual gesture is for real. He pulls out of my mouth and asks, "Do you know how long I've wanted to do this with you?"

"No, I don't." I sound ridiculous and nervous, out of my rainbow realm.

"Since you were eighteen ... Two years ago."

"And now what, Tag?" I ask, totally at a loss for movements and actions, but easily willed to attempt whatever the Spanish-speaking god inspires.

It's too late for him to respond, though. Tag is already on his knees. He capsizes his firm and sucking lips over my rod, presses the college-toy into the passage of his mouth, consuming its head and shaft, and even some brown strings of pubes that twist above my Alisar-food.

I pump the seven inches of firm post into his mouth as he gulps for air. He can't seem to control the exploitative thrusting into his saliva-cove. A man-scented perspiration begins to cling to the insides of my thighs as he slips hands up and under my T-shirt, and begins to twist on taut nipples and brass-like pecs. Above him, I moan, "Tag, Tag ... you're going to make me ..."

Someone's coming (and it's almost my creamy and gooey load into the back of Tag's opened mouth). I hear expensive heels click on oak stairs, climbing towards us, becoming louder and closer. It's Mrs. Snotty-Pissy Wellington who is back from her afternoon game of bridge.

I try to pull away from him, but can't. Tag's mouth is clamped to my flesh-rocket. I push on his naked shoulders and murmur, "Off, Tag ... off."

If Tag Alisar doesn't rise from his knees and pull off my extension of veined throat-pumper, unable to give me the five seconds I need to pull up my jeans and zipper, then we are majorly fucked by the old cow who is working her way up the stairs and into her bedroom, finding us in our compromised position.

Tag's good, though, simply bolts off my rod, and immediately stands up. He wipes the back of his right palm across his mouth, and quickly pulls up his jeans, buttoning them closed.

I'm not far behind, instantaneously pull up my own jeans, zip up tight, and stare dumbly at a pleased Mrs. Wellington. She approves and compliments our work. Wellington says with excitement, "Oh how wonderful ... You boys are polishing!"

We smile innocently, reply, "Yes ... of course." Wellington leaves us to finish our work. We finalize some matters with the furniture, finish polishing her dresser, slide the writing desk a little bit to the right, and create other necessary changes for improvement.

About two minutes after Wellington's departure, it's Tag who slips up beside me, presses his still-swelled package into my own, bear hugs me with his titanic biceps, and kisses my neck like a vampire in heat. He pulls off eventually and implores, "I'm not done with you yet, Timmy."

I attempt to push him away, but fail miserably, and scold him, "Not here, Tag, she'll come back."

"Then let's get out of here so I can finish what I started with you, Lift."

He starts where he leaves off. Alisar drives the truck behind the nearest Home Depot and promptly tells me to climb into the back. There's a few more pieces of furniture in the back (McIntrye chaise-lounge with pull-out sofa bed, an art deco enamel kitchen table from 1925, and a five drawer Berkey and Gay highboy dresser made of crotched walnut with brass knobs) that belongs to a gay couple on Supner Avenue—our second delivery for the day.

As the risky, wild, and horny Tag shuts the rear man-door to the truck, closing us in, he clicks on a twelve volt battery operated flashlight that illuminates the tomb-like area with dim light. I see his pointed nipples and rippled chest, the thin line of dark hair that floods into his jeans around his navel. He stands a few feet away from me and questions, "What's our company's motto, Timmy."

"We treat your valuables with kid-gloves."

The ex-Navy man chuckles, "Exactly," and flushes towards me, pressing my back into the walnut dresser, quickly pulling my tee over shoulders and dropping it to the truck's floor near dusty furniture covers. His tongue rushes to my right nipple and pec as his free fingers pull my zipper down. Tag breathes heavily over me, filling the compartment with a light, audible groan. The Latino's skilled and moving hands undress me with ease, drop jeans to floor, and tease my cock to a new, stiffening life.

We kiss like boyfriends. Alisar slips his tongue into the back of my throat, and I do the same with him. He treats me with kid gloves, massages my cock and balls, teases my lips, earlobes, and nipples, leaving me to think: *I'm literally swept away by Tag Alisar.*

It almost seems sensible to use the chaise-lounge for our continued dance, but to no avail, we use the chest of drawers instead. The heated and fiery man stands completely naked in the ass-end of the truck with his pumped legs spread, and his back against the chest of drawers. He begs, "Suck it, Lift … I want to fuck your mouth."

I've desired this single moment for as long my Latino friend has. There have been heated and uncomfortable summers that I have worked side-by-side with Tag, finding it utterly difficult from keeping my brown eyes off his deliciously-molded body, steering my hands away from his dick-jolting biceps, slippery thighs, and carved chest. And now, drawing my body towards his, clasping my swelled man-pointer to his beckoning Lift-teaser, I lick the cords in his neck, a bullet-like nipple, and the ridges lining his ab-covered torso. With ease, I decide that it is worth all those innocent summers for this mere moment with Tag Alisar, that it is nothing less than a sinful act of idolization.

I'm on my knees and comprehend that his hard and vein-thumping beam doesn't fit entirely into my mouth because it's far too long and wide. I believe that I'm only capable of gliding four inches between my lips, sucking masterfully on Tag's tool. I manage five, though, and then a surprising six inches. With a working tongue, I lap at the mushroom head and muscle-lines on his cock. He goes crazy above me, calls out my name with a frenzy. Tag moans and groans like an unpredictable animal on the loose. He runs tender hands through my blond hair and over my shoulders, and delicately pinches my nipples as if they are power knobs, controlling our rapid speed, attempting to increase our moment from FAST to FASTER.

I have him right where I want and need him, where I have always wanted and needed him. And just before he is willed to fire off his creamy, bitter, and salty load into my mouth, Tag pulls out of me and heads for his left-behind jeans. Upon his travels, he instructs, "Your turn, Lift."

"My turn?"

"You'll see. Pull out the second drawer from the bottom ... I've got a surprise for you."

We are mere shadows in the back of the truck. One is hulking and muscular, and the other is somewhat smaller but still absorbingly attractive.

Tag is back in a flash, holds a large sized, plastic condom in his right hand. "Turn around and cock your left leg up onto the drawer, Timmy. It's time to lock this contract together."

"Contract?"

He slips the tip of his ass-finder against me, presses the head inside my ass, and begins to spread me apart, holding onto my narrow hips.

"Hang on, Lift ... We're just getting started."

I reach for part of the dresser's top, hold on for dear life as Alisar pushes three more of his solid eight inches into my gay-chute. I choke without having anything in my mouth. His probing, digging, and thumping meat works my ass apart, feels as if it is pushing against the back of my throat. I feel dizzy and weak over the dresser, hang on tight, keep my balance, feel his pulverizing and thrusting man-blasts. Tag, I realize, has his entire knob in my delivery truck, is taking inventory of my insides, and is polishing the goods. I can't move in front of him, I can only wail with excited and warm pain as he relishes the smoothness of my interior-ass.

He sounds as if he is hyperventilating behind me. As Tag continues to pop his shaft into my ass, pulling out, pushing in again, causing a state of delirium to settle within my mind, he calls over my right shoulder, still hanging onto my hips, "Time for your show, Lift ... I'm pulling out."

Tag does what he says by dropping his hands first. He impulsively pulls his rod out of my used chamber, and spins me around. I watch him fling the gooey condom to the truck's floorboards, and listen to the Latino-man whisper (with a glazed look of satisfaction skiing across his face), "Wash me with your load, Lift."

I'm thrusting hips into cock as Tag does the same. It is mere truck harmony as we polish our cocks off, finishing what we've started. It is mere teamwork between men, gay-wonderment, and masculine ecstasy that is shared.

He strokes his cock like a madman, up and down, using both hands. If I don't already know any better, I can easily guess he is a star in pornographic movies, saving his burst for the right moment, expanding on his intentions, unconditionally willed to wash me with his stinging-hot goo. Tag chants, "The polish is coming, man."

I smile at him as we face each other. With a few more strokes to his beef, I feel his Peruvian-load shoot out of his cannon-like ass-digger and onto my solid cock and nicely developed chest, stiff nipples and chin.

An infatuating rush overcomes my body. As I finger pulsating blaster, breathing heavily, having my chest rise and fall, cheeks flushing and ass still burning from Tag's impulsive ride, I can't help myself any longer. With both hands, I gather up Tag's cock-juice. My right hand uses the Latino-syrup as lubricant on my steel dolly, and my left hand merely spoons the tasty globs of Tag-rush into the fragment of my mouth. With both actions I become inebriated and mesmerized, and unexpectedly ejaculate my liquidy and sweet Lift-sap from my steeping, ready-to-explode protein.

Just before I spout my pressurized blast, Tag Alisar surprises me by dropping to his knees. He opens his mouth for my expected treat, accepting the banquet with honors. I direct the flow into his opened cavern, gagging him with the immediate eruption, and then spraying his chin and chest, and both dimples and cheeks with the remaining load, becoming spent with him.

And there in the dark truck with flashlight, and a heavily breathing, sticky Tag Alisar, I whisper, "Do you have to move to Arizona, Tag? Can't you stay here?"

He looks over at me with his dim-colored, amethyst eyes, and smiles. Tag Alisar leans into me, and seals us together as newfound boyfriends with an impressive kiss, chants, "I'm all yours, Timmy Lift ... and I'm not moving anywhere."

I kiss Tag back, smile, and think: *He's found me ... Tag is perfect and rough, but just right. And now he's mine.*

MOONLUST

~ ~ ~

Brush Hellton is the big, bulky, and smooth looking Ukrainian man that is totally obsessed with me. He works down at The Legend's Carnival in Ruthingford Field, a fourteen day event in my small, New England college town. I don't know him, but half of me wants to. I'm interested in his strong muscles, thick thighs, and his darkly alluring good looks. And yes, I've been watching him as much as Brush has been watching me: Brush in the park and under the moonlight rays, stalking innocent and pertinent me with his shirt slightly gaping, showing off perfectly constructed abs and pecs, chasing after me as if I am prey; Brush bathing in the nearby river, diving up and down, showing hidden-me his bulbous sliver of delicious looking ass; Brush secretly masturbating behind the campus gym, stroking off eight inches of tool with both hands, speedily and ferociously, with neck arched and gritting teeth, bursting a load onto his splay of hairless, muscled chest, groaning in an untamed manner.

And once during his fourteen-day stay, we come very close to each other, head-on, twenty-eight year old carousel operator with eighteen year old Emberton College freshman,

128

our different worlds collide, smash together, and connect in Waterman Hall. I return from taking a shower down the hall. My roommate is out jogging, and I walk into my dorm room with nothing more than a gray cotton towel wrapped loosely around my waist. A mini-bucket swings from my right hand filled with Dial soap, Prell shampoo, and a Mach 3 razor. I close the door behind me and exhale with shock while accidentally dropping the bucket to the dorm room's floor, my towel following behind. I say with surprise, "What are you doing in here?"

Brush Hellton is too stunned to say anything, too possessed with my handsome body as he merely stands in my dorm room with both hands pivoted over his jean-covered private parts, a look of shameless awe smeared over his gallantly mysterious, and traveling-man face. He has a second or two to take my body in and drool over me: hairless and thin chest that is decorated with tiny nipples and gently crafted, light-weight abs; blonde and curly tuft of hair between striking legs; thin and glistening still-wet shaft dangling with two round, nicely packaged balls in extra skin. Brush, I see, licks his bloody-colored lips once, and then twice before he bolts, preventing me from obtaining an answer.

He knows about rules and regulations, principles and laws, yet human nature has caused him to break moral means by intruding and invading my personal dorm room. I could call the cops, imprison him, find him to be ruthless and unclean, a filthy road-traveling man that is completely unfit for the student body at Emberton College, yet perfect for my body at Victorian-styled Waterman Hall.

Instead, I'm turned on by his mysterious invasion into my private, virginal world away from my innocent home in Nashville, Tennessee. I like what has happened, and only desire to continue our secret, perhaps romantically scathing and dangerous game.

I'm in control. Brush doesn't know who he's spying on. He doesn't understand or comprehend my strong attachment to and for him. Once again, I escape the dorm room and head down to The Legend's Carnival in Ruthingford Field. I see the Ferris Wheel with all its circular splendor and nightly rainbow lights; vendors stand at hot dog and cotton candy carts; jugglers spin bottles on heads, palms, and feet as clowns sell balloons or stringed puppets. There is the Rocket Ride, two capsules that hold four riders each, spinning in opposite, vertical circles. Chaotic screams burst from the Fun House as spendthrift boys play mindless, thieving games for stuffed prizes and secret kisses from their sidekick boyfriends. Everything is magical and spectacular, but nothing is as glorious, sensual, and striking as the carousel operator.

Yes, the hand-carved, gold-trimmed, and elaborate designs of the carousel horses are a breathtaking vision. The horses are gentile and colorful, immortal looking with their harmless bits and reins, spinning with pride, glowing in the night. And yes, the music that blares into the college-indulged town is miraculously appealing with its harmonic sound and old-fashioned eloquence. But it is the man behind the operation that I'm fully attracted to: charcoal colored crew-cut glowing in the spiritual and glittery rainbow-light, firm jaws and narrow reddish lips, nicely trimmed mustache and goatee, tight T-shirt clinging to a bulky upper-frame that sports wrestler-sized pecs and knoblike nipples. My eyes peruse the carousel operator with questionable need and a longing that is intensified with a monastic fire.

I hand Brush my three tickets for his ride, lock my eyes with his sinister ones, and slowly smile, diving into his questionable, darker world.

He brushes two fingers against the back of my hand as he takes the tickets, rips them in half, and tosses them into a plastic bucket. He charmingly sneers at me, whispers, "We meet again, my friend. I'm glad you came to see me."

I don't answer him, press forward, and step up onto the white boards that make up the circular plane holding the carousel horses. And once positioned on an elaborately designed horse, blue and gold in color, front hooves splaying up and forward, leather belt strapped around my waist, aluminum pole pressed between khaki colored cargo pants, and tight reins locked into firm hands, the ride begins.

Loud, instrumental music plays; it's from *The Phantom of the Opera*. It's perfectly melodramatic music that offers a romantic-smoothness on this wispy and chilly evening ride with the carousel operator nearby, watching me spin around and around on my gold-blue horse. I connect eyes with Brush as my hand-crafted horse rises and falls, still moving around and around. He's seated on a tiny, oak stool with his legs slightly spread. His flawlessly onyx colored eyes are mystical and alluring, dissolve in my young masculinity. Around and around the carousel spins. Brush does a quick study of my body: mid-sized biceps bulging as strong hands tightly grasp long pole between somewhat hardening thighs, narrow feet planted into brass stirrups, flat stomach and just-right ripples on chest.

Slowly, the carousel stops, but the music continues. I'm about to unleash the belt from my waist when Brush comes up to my side. His face is the same height as my right thigh, and his massive Ukrainian hands clamp over my palms against pole. The dark and mysterious man asks, "Did you enjoy your ride, Luke Catta?'

"How do you know my name?" Brush catches me off guard.

He's gentle, caring, and tingly-hot. "I know a lot about you. Don't be frightened of me." I feel him reach for the leather contraption around my waist as Brush tenderly frees me.

"I'm not," I answer, swing one leg over the horse, sitting side-saddle with my legs now slightly opened.

Brush responds by merely dipping his head forward, placing nose, red lips, and tongue against my khaki-covered package, breathing me in, licking me, and kissing the thin fabric, causing me to grow firm between my legs, stinging me with absolute silence.

I'm spinning around and around on top of the wooden horse, but the carousel isn't moving. The pole between my legs swells to an obnoxious proportion almost immediately, prompts a devilish pre-pop of goo to erupt in my cargo's. I feel nervous and dizzy as the Ukrainian quickly operates my private part.

His head stays in the V-area of my crotch for over five seconds, becomes lost there, busy and engrossed, occupied to the fullest of craving-activities. When he pulls off, which feels like an eternity, he directly says, "You're innocent, aren't you?"

"Yes," I breathe in and out.

"And you've never been kissed, right?"

"Never." I shake my head. Not by a girl or guy. No one.

Brush smiles up at me, responds, "That's what I thought," and begins to help me down by placing his hands on my firm hips. He says, "Go ahead and slip off, Luke, I'll catch you."

I do as he says, allow gravity to consume my body against his. The swelled seven inches of my crotch meets his handsome face again, burrowing next to his skin and facial hair. And slowly, like maple syrup being tapped from a Vermont tree, I slip down along his body, having his tongue and lips and goatee meet my shirt-covered navel, abs, and the center of my hard pecs. As our crotches slip together, our mouths are only inches apart. There are strangers everywhere though, and we cannot kiss, deploy lips against lips. We are different, untamed, and secretly enflamed for each other. Grounded, I stand against him with my cock buzzing against his own, and whisper, "Thanks."

"You'll come back for another ride, I hope." Bush has an enigmatic luster in his charming and strangely debonair eyes. He smiles at me, caressing my stomach with his right palm, gliding the palm up and along my chest, over a taut nipple, and then the length of my neck, ending the journey of his traveling fingers on my mouth, caressing fingertips to narrow and slightly parted lips that need, desire, and want to do nothing less than to kiss his divine skin.

"Tomorrow night," I whisper. "I have enough tickets for one more ride."

His smile is bliss-filled and meaningful, something a young boy of eighteen will never forget for the rest of his life. Brush unquestionably hums, "You won't disappoint me, Luke, right?"

Before escaping back to Waterman Hall, dashing through a welcoming fog and untamed bats that are common to the college campus, I say to the roving and visiting stranger, "I'll be here," feeling tingly and bubbly all over, nervous and unusually careless, poetically lighter, too.

How do I feel inside? Why am I spirited with thoughts of Brush's lips against my own, his slim nose caressing the fabric of my cargo pants? Why can't I concentrate on homework and exams and reading/analyzing Ray Bradbury's boyishly-erotic novel *Something Wicked This Way Comes*? I become lost and confused. My world spins around and around like a carousel, and I believe nothing will settle the dragonflies or spirited sparrows that glide and flutter within my stomach. I become hooked on a single amusement ride and a dashing stranger who possibly has the ability to unfailingly fulfill a young man's freshman semester with intoxicating ecstasy.

The darkness and dreaminess of Waterman Hall consumes me. I study, bathe, and eventually turn to sleep. And here, tucked in the misty layers of my dreams I meet Brush Hellton again. He amazingly unlocks my dorm room, glides inside, and peels his stern body free of its clothes. I listen to him say, "I've missed you, Luke."

I desire nothing less than for him to slide over to my bed and still body, pull the sheets back, and slip next to me. My eyes connect with his long, slivered legs and the massive tube of nightly cock dropping between them. I concentrate on his movements as he takes one, massive palm and diligently presses it against his lower-stomach, slowly gliding the palm up and along his sculpted chest, higher and higher, until he reaches his slightly opened mouth where, one by one, he licks each of his fingertips with an outstretched, amber tongue.

Tucked in the gray-black folds of my dream, I ask, "What are you doing here?"

Brush removes saliva from his parted lips and pulls at the length of his hanging sword. He stares at me with his hypnotic, spell-forming eyes, and recites rather sentimentally, "I'm here to turn you into a man, Luke. Don't be afraid of me. Don't be shy. I won't hurt you." And slowly he moves across the granite floor and puffy fog that has somehow entered the bedroom, and slips into my bed, pulling silken red sheets over our head, concealing our like bodies as we devise an immortal kiss between student and stranger.

I sleep through the day. When night is welcomed, I rise. It's after ten o'clock and I realize that the carnival will be closing soon. School boys and girls have already headed back to their chapel-like dorms for sleep or to study, or to attend rambunctious and erotically shadowy parties in vast mausoleum-like abodes until the break of clustering dawn. I shower and dress, spray on a sweet masculine cologne and head down to Ruthingford Field in hopes of finding Brush Hellton.

I'm two blocks away from Emberton's campus when I realize that someone's following me. I bolt to the left down Ransom Way, and then to the right across Peddler Drive, and end up dashing into the Emberton Cemetery. Ruthingford Field is on the other side of the cemetery, I know. This is a shortcut that even the strongest, gutsiest, and rock-hard jocks don't even take at night. Quickly, I run past tombstones, granite angels kneeling over graves, and freshly unearthed graves. The cold fog languidly drapes around my ankles and slows me down. I become faint and out of breath, stop and lean into one of the massive, sky-reaching adamantine mausoleums. My heart is pounding and I need to get back to my dorm where there is light, warmth, and a sense of saintly comfort. I'm a fool for coming out on my own, facing night, darkness, and ...

Out of nowhere something presses against my mouth and chest, between my legs, startling me. I feel warmth between my lips, pressure against my khaki-covered cock. The repression eventually releases and I hear Brush Hellton whisper over-top me, "I've been expecting you, Luke."

I'm shivering under his nightfall spell. "I'm a little late ... I'm sorry."

He longs to be connected to me, I sense. Here in the game of night, autumn around us with crisp leaves and a lazy fog, with a full moon blooming overhead, forecasting a gothic embrace between the likeness of men, Brush whispers into my right ear, "I need you tonight, Luke."

Before I can utter a single response, he rolls his tongue up and along my right cheek, gently cups my package with his left hand, hardening up my evening goods, and whispers in the chilly, moonlit shadows, "It's okay, I completely understand that you're frightened. You don't need to be, though. I'm here to please you, Luke. Trust me."

I say things I can't comprehend. Brush kisses me hard, separating my lips. I become easily drained by his tongue in my mouthy tomb. After a state of nice delirium is disposed of between us, his hands quickly ditch my clothes. And after drowning me in hot and fiery kisses, pulling dark clothes from his slim and erotically eye-cleansing body, Brush instructs, "Turn around, Luke."

I am helpless against his concoction of eighteen year old need. Expectedly, I spin around and place my palms on the stone mausoleum as Brush gently pats my legs apart, allowing my balls and stiffening cock to droop romantically between shivering legs. In the distance I can hear the carousel's music. It's music of the night that drains into my ears. Wind carries the enchanting melody to our mausoleum enclosure, wrapping around our naked bodies. With utter surprise, though, the music and elaborate wind is forgotten. Brush begins to roll his tongue and lips over my untouched, backside cheeks. The feeling is warm and cozy--meant to be between boy and man in Emberton Cemetery. As I crane my neck, allowing his movements to control me with fervent bliss, I feel his tongue enter and exit me, light and prosaic darts of flesh meeting inner-boy-core, gently opening a virginal door to my soul.

The moistened and warm touch of his tongue against my dormant innocence continues. Brush growls and groans behind me, diving into me, harboring half of his face into my newly opened depths. He breathes like an animal, grunting wildly, pushing and pressing his mouth-sliver into my burning and now semi-released desire. And slowly, with skill and utter grace, like a melancholic opera unfolding before us, Brush spins me around, laps at my chest and nipples with his busy and mastering tongue, pivots his face against my navel, and the triangle-blonde curls that look brown in the undercurrents of dismal moonlight. A heavily breathing Brush emphatically worships my eight inch protrusion of freshman-wonder, lapping at its bulbous head and excess skin, slipping tongue and teeth against its unexplored veins, working the Brush-teaser as if it a device or lever to control a magical carousel ride between uncivilized men and their forbidden connections.

I'm not in control; I have never been in control with Brush Hellton. I decide this as he whispers words into the fog-clenched night: *fresh, unscathed,* and *pure.* Brush slowly devours my manly spike, teasing me, causing me to feel lost and broken, yet completely groundless, lifted by his mouthy pleasure. I groan in an uncivilized manner in the night, like an angry and hungry wolf needing flesh and contentment. A loss of control comes over me as I gently push his head away, demanding innocently, "Stop ... just stop! It's going to be over if you don't"

Brush understands my every whim of desire and releases his soft mouth from my fleshy inflammation. As our eyes lock together, I can see his evening appetite. I scan his body with my own discovered longing: hardened and sweaty pectorals; V-enchanting legs sprouting a massive, ten inch stake; medicinal-like balls dangling in the evening moonlight like idolized, masculine planets. I whisper, "You're beautiful."

He responds contritely, "I know," and pulls me towards his steepingly warm body in the chilly, autumnal glow, whispering, "I'll be careful with you, Luke ... Trust me." Without hesitation he gently tows me away from the mausoleum and pushes down on my shoulders, my stomach, connecting my back to the straw-like grass of fall, the moon rising and rising, becoming more clear and heavy and wide, chanting again and again, "You've always dreamed of me, Luke. This is what you want."

And here on the burnt grass, leftovers of a heated and ardent summer, the carousel man kneels over-top me, positioning a lubricated condom onto his nightly and mechanical poker that he has easily retrieved from his jeans. He smiles down at a less innocent me staring up into his soothing and avant-garde eyes. With skill, the stranger from The Legend's Carnival hoists my right leg up onto his strong shelflike shoulder. He explains quite compassionately, "Expect a little pain, my new friend."

Before I can comprehend what he is saying ... before I can rationally digest what is happening to a young boy of eighteen ... I feel his strong and throbbing inches enter me, causing me to yell out into the night, causing tears to rush into the corners of my eyes. I'm becoming separated by him: man from boy. It's painful and haunting yet enjoyable at the same time as he continues to push inch after inch of the condom covered spike into my insides, whispering and chanting and humming soliloquies above me, pushing deeper and deeper into me, driving the boy away, welcoming a man, leaving me to feel numb, content, and real for the very first time in my life.

It's as if I am on a carnival ride with him, spinning around and around, out of control, spiraling and revolving with Brush Hellton. Loud, instrumental music plays; it's from *The Phantom of the Opera,* again! It's perfectly melodramatic music that offers a romantic-smoothness on this wispy and chilly evening ride with the carousel operator inside me, watching me as if I am spinning in maddening circles on the length of his gold-blue horse. We connect eyes as my hand-crafted pony rises and falls between my legs with his fist-movement against its boyish skin, both of us twist and turn together ... thrusting, pushing, humping, and pressing into each other. He feels like an oak pole inside me with his legs slightly spread. His flawlessly onyx colored eyes are mystical and alluring above me, dissolve in my young masculinity. Helplessly our nightly carousel spins. Ferociously! Haphazardly! Our bodies cling together, freshman sealed to stranger ... a celebration of moonlust between us.

It's too late to question our positions in the graveyard. It's too late to turn back. He thrusts inside me again, growling at the moon and our passion, profusely sweating on my lower-stomach. Brush pulls out quickly and tosses the condom to the side. He flings his maddening hands against his post, working it up and down with a nocturnal rhythm, exploding white juts of stranger-spew into the night, filling the sky with guy-stars or white-winged moths taking off into flight, higher and higher, and then eventually losing control, spinning downwards, into earth, landing on my nipples and pecs, my cheeks and forehead, costuming my skin for Halloween.

And Brush, who is a heaving and sweaty pillar of used man above me, who I become sexually devoted to and have fallen for completely, stays between my spread legs, throttles my spear into his right hand, leans over me seductively and sweetly, smiles down at me, and whispers, "Give something up in the bone yard, Luke ... I can't wait any longer."

138

As he rocks my eight inches of tool up and down, I feel lighter and captivated by his touch. The half-hidden moon spins crazily above me as clouds seem to stampede by in the charcoal colored sky. A mist of fog tenderly blows over our connected bodies as cold breath escapes my opened mouth. One upwards thrust of my hips teases Brush. A second thrust of my hips, after speedy and consecutive strokes, frees a burning, eighteen year old load of boy-sap to fly out of my hose, spraying an over-excited and smiling Brush Hellton down with white, sticky, college-goo, dousing his upper torso, chin, and reddish lips.

Breathing heavily, his hulking chest rising and falling, Brush kisses me as if we will be immortal lovers throughout eternity. His come-stained lips caress my left shoulder, my earlobe, my parted and sensual lips. I will never see him again, will I? He's a ghost or spirit of some sort, an erotic traveler, the carousel keeper, the boy tamer, a man with needs and darkly lit fires. A spiritual, flesh-guide. I breathe him in slowly, softly, hold him until after midnight, when he finally has to return to his carousel and heaven ... somewhere ... and then he is gone, forever.

OFFICER, I DIDN'T MEAN TO

~ ~ ~

I see the blue/red/white lights from behind me in the rearview mirror, autumn all around, patrol lights that mix with red/yellow/orange. I say, "Shit!" obnoxiously. I don't want a ticket, but the odds are against me, and have always been against me. I have just blown through three red lights in the city. God and fate are out to get me.

It's a city cop. The worst of the worst. They are usually big, and have fear in their voices, or posted across their broad, hairy, and dark chests. I pull the bright red Mustang over to the right side of the road, flick on my four-ways, and gaze intoxicatingly into my rearview mirror with ease . . . perhaps even contentment.

The blue-purple sun is blocking the view of the pig behind me. I rub at my rock-hard cock in my jeans, try to push it away, but viewing the flashing lights is a total turn-on. I take a minute to prep, look into the rearview mirror at myself: vivid blue-violet eyes, chocolate colored skin, rough boy looks with an edge that is very wild and unrefined, gold hoop earrings, thick cords in my pumped neck from working out. Yes, I'm everything a cop wants. I'm bad-ass Arnell

Jackson with attitude and good looks, chiseled and perfect. A street God. The God with fly.

Cop is bigger than big: six three, wide as a truck on top, massive structured shoulders like some skyscraper. He has a very thin waist, thick thighs all packed into his gray trousers. Mr. Cop leans over and peers into my window at me through his silver, reflective lenses. His chest looks as if it is going to pop out of his gray uniform, breaking buttons and badge and packed heat. I see his clean Marine hair-cut, slicked back with gel, short and streaking black, very thin eyebrows. His eyes glow with an impromptu act of desire. Cop's slender, long nose is delicious looking, and his chin is round. He's about twenty-eight years old, well experienced, needed for a boy of eighteen like me to enjoy and mount and throttle and please and . . .

I look at his name badge. It glints silver and reads: T. Pound. I try to smile but can't, because fear of liking him too much settles into me and begins to take over my mind. Never have I locked onto a man so large and hulking. Pound can breathe on me and I will break into two queenly-pieces of dark niceness. Pound can press his crotch further into my face and I can . . .

"You know how many laws you just broke?" He keeps his eyes on my T-shirt-covered nipples.

I reply, "Officer, I didn't mean to."

My eyes catch on Pound's meat-filled crotch outside my opened window again. The mound causes me to lick my plump red-lined lips. I see his pistol beside outlined cock. I see handcuffs and his Billy club . . . or Arnell club. I can lick his slacks and hidden boy-pusher if I want to, that's how close Cop is. I can gently touch my tongue to his loaded, dark gun if he permits me to. I can . . .

"Bro, you could have killed someone going that fast."

"I was in a hurry . . . I don't know what I was thinking." The urge to reach out and touch his covered meat is conveniently overwhelming. I keep my place though, stay in the Mustang.

He gawks mysteriously at my hard cock in my jeans, licks his lips once, and pulls his glance away from me. Something questionable lurks in his behavior that makes my Cop-need twitch in my jeans. Pound asks with seriousness, "Do you know how much this fine is going to be?"

I'm too turned on by him to answer. I have the ability to see the future and I know he's going to sock it to me . . . whether with his tongue, the Arnell club, or his meat-probe, Cop is going to carry out some guy-nasty with me. I don't stand a chance in hell with this Black stud-guy and getting out of a ticket.

But I have to try to get out of this mess. He is going to take my license away from me, no doubt. Pound is going to ruin me. For now though, he keeps his eyes on my hard, ten inch slab of meat that is covered with denim as he looks from it to my sweaty forehead, boy-toy face, and chiseled chest. I use my goods and street-smarts attitude, and boyishly eighteen year old manner to obtain freedom, ask, "Really Officer, I didn't mean to. Can we talk about this? I'm sure there's a way of getting me off."

Shit! I say *getting* instead of *letting*, and now . . . now he's going to really plaster me with a ticket. Now Cop is going to . . .

He rubs his bulging and throttling cock though, reaches into the car with his hand and touches my lips with his massive fingers. Pound tells me to take a sniff of his fingers, and adds, "Is there a way to forget about this?"

"Why don't you just piss off?" It's the wrong thing to say to Mr. African-American Hottie with his badge on meaty, bulging plain of metal chest. I choke his happiness into suffocation. I bring out the worst in him.

He first tells me to get the fuck out of the Mustang, and secondly, he tells me to lean against the hood of the car, with hands pressed against metal, with back and hard ass facing him. Mr. Young Piss-Me-Off (*me!*) tries to obtain a sense of masculine freedom, but Pound manages to maintain my weight, presses me to the patrol car with his cock and hands against my lickable ass. He scurries the hands over every muscle on my body, giggling behind me in his naughty-ass tone. Cop pats me down with a skill that is crotch-hardening, informs, "Don't mess with me. I gotta see what I'm in for." T. Pound rolls fingers up and down my sides, reaches around me, presses the fingers into the bulging area of my crotch, carefully devotes his skills to my succulent, pleasurable and pleased body. He says, "Not bad . . . Not bad at all. Your bark is much worse than your bite. But we'll have to see about that."

T. Pound places my ripped body into the front seat of his patrol car by caressing my back and need-to-be touched rump, a soothing pleasure that drives me wild, informs me rather quickly and cleverly that I'm in for a hot ride tonight. "Make this easy on yourself, young man, okay?"

He caresses my shoulders, and then my back again, makes sure I'm safe in the patrol car. I stare out at him and say rather pleasantly for the very first time, "Yes, Sir ... I'll be on best behavior."

Pound escorts me to the parking lot behind the abandoned library across town. He has a hard-on in his uniform that won't let up. He leaves the handcuffs in the patrol car, parks, and retrieves me from my bliss-induced state of lust and greed. The officer of the law permits me to stand up against the closed, passenger's door with metal to my back as his piercing and vivid eyes melt me. He asks, "You wouldn't run away from me, right?"

"No, Sir ... Never. I'm a nice guy. Can't you see it in my eyes?"

He smiles and laughs. "I'll show you what I can see in your eyes, young man." Pounds lifts my T-shirt off of slippery abs and nicely crafted, youthful pecs. The bull takes a moment out to enjoy the evening and my body by rolling a single, massive finger down to one nipple, across my cinnamon colored abs, pushing his hand down into my jeans. He starts to play with Arnell's street goods next ... still smiling.

I mumble with unstoppable joy and heated lust, "Really, I didn't mean to speed back there. Can't you . . . can't you--"

He places two fingers on my lips, shoves one into my mouth, pulls it out, teasing me. Two new appendages pinch at my right nipple with short but quick strikes. Next, Cop begins to bite at the nipple, pulls it with his white, clean teeth, keeps preoccupied with my desiring flesh. I'm still needy for him, burning in my ass, craving his cock to maybe tease my hole with a sudden and delicious, rhythmic blast of cop movements. I realize quite easily that I'm barely able to move, though, completely lost and turned-on by Mr. Beefman in front of me. With skill, I gently roll my head back, allow the tiny sticks of hair on his pointed chin to caress my boy-delicious skin. Pound meanders his hand into my crotch, pushes my balls together with a cupped hand, and promotes me to groan out with gratification and qualified pleasure.

As he pulls his grip off my nipple with his bare teeth, Pound whispers, "This is part of your fine. You shouldn't have went that fast."

He doesn't give me time to answer, though. Pound dives back onto my nipple, yanks at it with gliding fingers, finds my covered package with the same speedy fingers, and deliberately turns me on, causing me to smoothly smile and begin to pay my dues for breaking laws.

Half of me wants to stay connected to him for the next twenty-five years, carry out a marriage with the Law. And the other half insists on licking nothing less than his evening meat-puppet, again and again. There are no options for me, though. Pound has an agenda of his own, is quite clear about proximities. I can tell rather plainly that T. Pound is bubbly for me, stung and hard, wishing for my hands to stroke him off, press fingers into his dark skin, clean his pumped body of the nicely pressed uniform that can easily be called sleek and well-designed for cop-body.

I play the game well. I've no other desires. My natural instinct to carry out this moment with the cop is ... rational. I answer him by saying, "I promise I won't go anywhere."

Pound listens, but he's apprehensive at first, gently frees me from the metal side of patrol car, presses me against his slick chest, sniffs my neck, licks my cheek, and carries out a masculine and power-induced kiss with my lips that causes a boy-rod to spurt a few drops of healthy pre-goo into my pants.

He's not done with me. Eighty percent of my mind understands that he has just started this guy-romp between us. Cop-God carefully rubs his uniformed covered cock against my lower torso, teasing me, just for a second, no more. Next, the sliver of Trojan-like man pulls me around and allows my fingers to unbutton his shirt, one by one, button by button.

As my heart drops to the pavement of the parking lot, I'm free to linger fingers over his sculpted chest. With a proficiency that is miraculous, I find his dark pecs that are the size of doorknobs, and squeeze each dramatically, turning him on more, causing the cop to grown mildly. Pound bucks his clothed thighs and cock into me, touches his hips to mine. He's ready and willed to create some sweet and intricately law-abiding motion with me. I peel his black belt away as he stands for me to undress him. He finds my face once, pulls my head to his dreamy eyes, cheeks, and lips, leaving our tongues to arrest each other in a contemptible condition of intoxicated, man-on-man bliss.

Cop pulls away and informs, "Laws aren't made to be broken."

I run hands along his bulky arms, through his black hair, and over sweaty-slick chest. His nipples glow with utter perfection as I caress the strands of fine hair that lead down into his gray slacks that mix with massive balls and cock. I touch his naval, one hip, and say for effect, "I shouldn't be doing this . . . I should be getting home. My mom will wonder where I am."

"You've got dues to pay. People break laws, there's sacrifices involved. You're not going anywhere until you're finished, man."

I play hard-boy, half-scared out of my naughty, acting mind. I pinch one of his nipples, then mine. I ask, "You don't plan on using the Billy club on me, do you?"

"Yes . . . That could get you off," he confesses, rolls his fingers over my lips, down into my jeans, finds my goods, measures them again by cupping the two fleshy orbs into his palm. Next, he frees his hand and pops my buttons loose on my jeans, unleashes the head of my slicked cock, a long dark shaft, and finally my dangling, free-for-all balls.

I piss him off by saying, "Keep your fucking queer hands off me, pig."

He chuckles. I'm his gay game and he knows it. I feel his hand squeeze my balls and cock, causing them to grow hard and harder. Pound says, "You're pussy ass is going to learn to show me some respect, bro. You understand that?"

My answer is simple and to the point, completely spirited with role playing. I don't even begin to comprehend that I will turn him on more. I don't know that he has every intention of laughing at me, playing with my body like some kind of road-toy. I say, "Are you going to give me a ticket or not?"

"You bet your ass," Cop responds--he isn't lying.

"You have the right to remain silent, queer. Anything you say or do will be held against you in *my* court of law."

"Fuck you," I breathe softly and roll my fingers through his thin hair, over his warm head, down his back. I challenge my fingers to touch every muscle in his back as he cups my balls hard, locks his fingers onto them, pulls with fiery need, beginning to crush them and . . .

"Criminal," he chants rather rudely, snickering lightly, driving me mad with erotic simplicity. "You need fucked, you know that?"

And I do. I need to feel all ten inches of his hard and hot flesh that he has to offer. I need my fine paid in full, and my asshole reamed out. Mercilessly, I mention, "I could have your badge for this."

It is the wrong thing to say in the right place. I piss Cop off even more, fire Pound up while listening to his heavy breathing. I immediately feel his slick, chocolate colored look against mine. His hidden cock becomes hard against my legs, and his long, reddish tongue and lips close over mine, and pull off quickly. His words sting me, like the essence of his cock: "I'm going to make you apologize for that, bro. You think you're fly . . . but you'll find out differently."

"You don't have the balls," I respond with a lie, because Cop's got the biggest balls I've ever touched.

"You want to know who's boss, don't you? You want to get stabbed by a big Cop?" He huffs and sinks his teeth into my nipple, my neck, one of my lips. I taste spit and high energy, everything that makes him butch and muscular, everything that fills him with steamy hot testosterone. "Lessons are to be learned tonight. Speeding lessons. Homo lessons."

My hands are slippery on the hood's fine surface. I become Pound's bait, his need, his evening meat-hole. He has me over the hood and I can't go anywhere--but I'm perfectly content with this action. Pound wants to find things hidden in my fuck-hole; maybe a weapon or something like that. I have nothing hidden there though, except for deep desire, and maybe tight and pink virgin ass-muscles to share with him.

And after he plugs me with two of his fingers minus the lube, finding nothing, making me hard like black steel,

Pound eventually rolls me over onto my back and balances me so my body won't fall off the car's hood, landing on the pavement below. He eyes me in a clever manner in the faded darkness, smiles with heated desire and cop-lust, whispers, "You should have never thought of speeding."

He doesn't give me time to answer. Instead, Pound spreads my legs wide and wider, and I feel both of his hands on my pecs, pinching my skin, pulling me towards him. I chant moderately with a meat-stem protruding from my middle, "You can't do this to me . . . I have rights."

"I'm doing my job, man. Don't start with me. You keep your position, and I'll do my job."

I have the right to remain silent.
I have the right to bear arms.
I have the right to . . .

I spread my legs wide for him, show off my clean ass for his eyes only. I feel sweat form all over my body as Pound's sleek shadow hangs over-top me. I become the prey that is in high demand, needing pleasure and cop-rod inside me, needing hot cop-cock up my slick ass. I become . . . the good citizen again.

Hard-cop Pound finally drops his pants. He is ready and willed to allow me to pay my fine, pay my dues to him-- *personally*. He snatches onto one ankle and holds it tight in his large hand, spreads my legs apart. He man-handles his ten inch dick with his other hand and moves his hips closer to the car, touches his drooping, Ping-Pong ball sized man-sack to the edge of the front hood--flesh against metal. He says gruffly, "Look at me while you pay your fine," and pinches his cockhead to the opening of my virgin-like, tight ass, pushing it into me . . . six inches, seven, eight . . . all of it, faster and faster, allowing it to lay in me with no lubrication. No spit. Raw cop-cock with condom and nothing more inside me. Cop-rod. Pig-sword. Black-boy-poker.

"Jesus," I whisper in pain, tense and hard on the hood, legs spread wide, with Pound inside me. He begins to push harder, pulls out with guy-suction, leaving me feel as if I am stoned and considerably numb.

"Jesus doesn't have anything to do with this," he says to me. "This is all about the law. This is treatment for speeders." Pound withdraws his meat-slab, but doesn't take it out the entire way. He shoves it quickly back into me, even harder this time, continuously, ramming me with every inch he has to offer, patrol-meat pushing into me, harboring within my fleshy tomb, at the base of my spine, at the ends of my stomach, at . . .

I can't move beneath him, feel crippled and lost. "Payment enclosed," I whisper out of mere wit, desire, and need. His chest is slicked with built-up sweat. His armpits smell ancient and masculine, meaty almost. He rocks inside me, bucks wildly, calls me names like: Race-boy, Metal-teaser, Cop-pleaser. Pound pumps it hard into me, as if it is the Billy club in his patrol car. He laughs harshly and proudly above me, with utter simplicity, "Take every inch of T. Pound . . . Make it last."

I scream with pleasure for the *real* police, but we're too hidden. I cry out for someone in the city to save me from his pumping and slamming, and out-of-line behavior, but no one's around; just Pound and his Poundee. Safety and performing.

He rushes into me again and again. His hips touch the back of my thighs. His balls smack off my tight ass. "This is what you want," he says once, his hand jutting up and down on my cock, prompting speedy vibrations to ripple through my body.

My hips buck up and down with his movement. My ass is consumed with his throbbing cock as he thrusts wildly within me, presses his ebony cock-hair against my balls. Pound arches his back, grins madly down at me. His nipples poke out into mid-air for me to leash onto as he begins to jerk me off with his pulling and finding cock-hands.

"You going to speed again?" he asks, slamming me hard.

"Yes, sir," I reply, grit my teeth, take everything he has to offer, pushing my dick into his moving hands, feeling his meat-grinder rock inside my man-ass.

I come first, though. Playing cop games in the evening is almost over. I whisper something I can't remember, keep hands locked onto Cop's nipples, thrust hips forward and up into his hand, feel his ass-pleaser push into me, more times than I can possibly imagine. Gooey white come flies out of the slit of my cockhead, sputters all over his thick chest, his navel, his nipples and lower neck. The whiteness of my come glints and hangs miraculously in the new evening as it drips off of Pound's torso in filthy strands. It glows in the dim twilight, shimmering.

Eventually, he releases his fingers from my stiff flag and keeps up his end of the bargain, gets ready to soak me wet with his man-juice as he prepares to spit it into the condom--and me--from his slut-staff.

After bucking into me, pressing my legs farther and farther apart, T. Pound writhes above me, and inside me. He creates one last pump with tedious care, shoves all of his radar love into me, pushing my insides apart, attempting to break me, scold me, fine me . . .

I feel his bubbling man-fluid fill me with the condom, swell with bulbous Godspeed. I feel sweat drip out the edges of my ass crack as T. Pound says something above me that I can't understand, something that is cop-talk, numbers or something like that that he uses on his CB.

As I rub my white dream-boy come into his plain of muscled chest, he smiles and grits his teeth at me, and chants, "Take all of it." Pound catches me off guard by bucking his hips again and again, filling me with him, flooding me with his hot, steamy spew-filled condom as his fingerprints lay around my ankles and come drips off his nipples and abs.

"How much more?" I groan beneath him, ready to give in. I feel him pull out with one quick motion. His shaft is smeared with parts of me and him. And my ass cheeks hurt like hell as he leaves me shiver on the patrol car's hood.

I am sweating and out of breath, lay listening to our breathing and the city.

"You meant to speed, didn't you?"

"Officer, I really *did* mean to."

And T. Pound shoves his tongue down my throat, clasping my neck and head to the hood of his patrol car as I latch his head with both of my hands, willed to kiss him hard with sex-driven need, again and again.

STROKIN' IT

~ ~ ~

Minimal and masculine groaning sounds surface in the gloomy distance. I'm in the rowing equipment shed on a Saturday morning, willed to prepare and ready equipment for my Nestleton College rowing team. Something surprises me though, completely catches me off guard. In the shadowy expanse, beyond the tiny area where First Aid kits are stashed, beyond a closet filled with wrist tape and other handy rowing supplies, the heated and animal-like sounds grow stronger and more steady. Slowly, I move forward, pass the arrangement of slim shell boats, the Spaulding life-jackets, and then abruptly pause. I hear slurping in the distance. It's a summer-type of slurping—like lips and mouth meeting watermelon. Patiently, I continue my steps and eventually stop at the red-and-white plastic buoys that we use for practice in the river. They hang down from iron ceiling hooks, keep me secluded and hidden. Precisely, obsessively, and diligently I stare between the hanging orbs with utter shock collecting in my mind, and a hardness that abruptly consumes my tantalized cock, leaving me to think: What's going on in here? ... Shame on me for intruding.

It's here in the hidden secrecy of the equipment shed where I'm supposed to turn away and leave at once. I can't, though. As I slip my right palm into gray sweats, wrapping fingers around meaty-buoy, totally astonished at the site in the equipment shed, I lick lips and listen closely to the distant slurping.

In the alluring distance, delicious Hunter Reed's in the equipment shed. He's the senior star rower, twenty-three years old and darkly handsome. Pure Italian with perfectly trimmed sideburns, melting amethyst colored eyes. He's physically beautiful with his model-like biceps and abs, a rowing god before me that is naked, facing me, and seated on the wooden table where we keep the oars. The oars are in a pile on the floor now, nicely and conveniently arranged. Hunter has his legs spread wide open, sporting an eleven inch, uncut splinter with corded veins, offering a bubbly surprise to flood through my body.

What transpires with my soft cock is nothing shocking. An appealing attraction to the head rower hosts itself to my mid-section and causes a teasing vibration to skirt down and through my sleeping Hunter-probe, bringing it to hard life. As my hand busies itself with splinter, I watch Hunter spread his legs wide and wider, showing off triangular pubic hair the color of coal, crisply cut abs, nicely developed chest, and perfectly sweet nipples.

The slurping sounds become louder and louder in the hidden area. I can't believe what I'm seeing. Hunter arches forward between his legs with a gymnast's skill, open mouth and seemingly craving lips, and laps at the bulbous and uncut length of his own pleaser. Tongue pivots against cock-hole, pulls off. Lips and saliva collect around meat-tube as back and neck concisely move forward, as head continuously bobs up and down. The rower is sucking himself off! Hunter's carrying out his own self-pleasure!

He doesn't see me behind the hanging buoys. While my hand busies itself in the sweats, rolling fingertips over eight inches of hardened staff, I become mesmerized by

Hunter's movements, self-blowjob in progress, an uncanny and erotic site that is pleasing to a coach's addictive and assertive eye. Tongue continues to lap at Hunter-cock as lips fall and rise over the steeping steam. Hunter looks stinging and hot, rapturous, delicious, and spine-tingling. A champion in all aspects of the word.

Eventually he stops blowing himself. The slurping sounds seize—I assume all good things must come to an end. And gradually, Hunter moves his left palm to the extension of eleven inches, wrapping it around meaty veins. Next, the right palm joins the left. And hand over hand—rhythmic beauty—he manipulates his stinging shaft, again and again, up and down, harmoniously, until Hunter can't keep his load in; until Hunter rises his hips in a bolting action, stupendously, higher and higher, falling, lifting again and again; until hot liquid spins, twirls, and sprays out of his man-pumper. The pungent juice burns his torso, navel, and the hard and rippled skin of his lower chest. Three consecutive arcs of man-sap fire from his wood and decorate Hunter's glowing and sweat-slippery skin. With ease he arches his neck back in satisfaction, humming a sensual sound of deep pleasure that is very similar to grunting. Hunter bucks his hips once, twice, three times, allowing more sap to flush out of his spike, enameling his precious and delicious skin ... becoming intoxicatingly and perhaps deliriously spent.

And sitting there naked and used on the table where we have negotiated team plays and configurations, game plans to winning a seasonal championship on the Hudson River, I watch intensely as Hunter admires the exuberant glow and masculine gleam of his chiseled chest. He's depleted and satisfied but doesn't know what to do with the pools and dribbles of glistening spew on his chest. There are no rags or towels nearby, nothing handy. Quickly, and with utter skill, he scoops up the liquidy mass from his lined abs with three fingers and immediately shoves the appendages into his opened mouth, two-knuckle deep. Again and again

Hunter Reed uses the fingers as tools, feeding himself the white goo, smiling with satisfaction—once again, a champion.

As my own right hand goes to town on coach-goods, I whisper uncontrollably, "Sooooooo hot."

With sudden surprise, Hunter lifts his blissful stare to the hanging, plastic buoys. Immediately he calls out, "Coach Galin? ... Galin ... is that you?"

I'm quiet and hidden. Neck cords firm up. Eyes grow wide and wider. The hand between my legs is preoccupied with its own feisty actions that are continuous. And eventually, pulsing with an inferno of sweat on my forehead, unable to fend off the expected and approaching orgasm that a coach occasionally finds athletically cleansing, fingers feel sticky jizm flush out the Hunter-find. I clamp lips closed and tightly clench teeth together, begin to buzz with my own orgasm, bursting a warm and gooey load into cotton sweats.

Out of nowhere a succulent and fiery Hunter appears. He's naked and standing on the other side of the plastic orbs. Slowly he reaches forward and separates the hanging buoys, questions, "Coach Galin?" His purplish eyes fall to the hand in my sweats. "What's going on?"

I say rather presumptuously, "I should ask you the same question, Hunter."

"You were watching me, weren't you?"

I smile over at his hulking shoulders, collect his eyes within mine, and reply indignantly, "Hunter, if you won't tell ... I won't tell."

With utter surprise he adds, "Tell what?"

"Your games in here ... You know perfectly well what I'm talking about."

The Italian god catches me off guard yet again. With superhero speed he glides towards me. Hunter closes his left palm around my right wrist and draws my fingers up to the sliver of my mouth. With need and a spontaneous action, the dark haired man slips two of the fingers into my mouth, and then a third. He pleasingly watches me lap up my man-spent, desiring its bittersweet taste. Quickly, he pulls the fingers out, drops my hand, leashes the back of my head with his right palm and draws me towards him, sealing his mouth to my pulsating neck, kissing me like a man and not a boy.

He pulls off, questions, "You won't say a word about us, right?"

I am too stunned to answer. I am left to do nothing more than shake my head and watch him collect his white shorts and shirt near the organized oars. I stand and stare at Hunter Reed as he dresses, steps up to me one last time before departing the equipment shed. Poetically he pulls me towards him, breathes on my neck and earlobe, whispering into my ear, "I'm not gay ... but I like you, coach. Let's keep this *our* secret."

Six days later, the call comes out of the blue on a Friday evening at my Nestleton office. "Coach, Galin?"

"Hunter?" I say his name, trying to conceal how he catches me off guard.

"I need a favor from you." He sounds nervous and strangely out his mundane sorts.

I sit back in my chair as far as it will go, kick my feet up onto the edge of my mahogany desk, spread my legs, and run a hand down the splay of my solid chest. Quickly, I tug up on my white Henley, cross fingers over polished and inflated abs, head southward bound with the straying fingers, and find the package between my legs. It's here in the valley of my Hunter-temptation where I concoct a spell of naughty guy-bliss inside my mind. I dream of pressing Hunter's ass cheeks apart, licking him clean, diving tongue and lips against the opening of his man-need, deeper and deeper, spreading him apart, filling him with a part of my soul, charisma, and dude-joy ... again and again and again!

"Galin?"

I've drifted; shame on me. "I'm here." My right hand works buttons free on my skin-tight shorts, and within seconds I have my eight hard inches of buddy out, immediately begin to roll fingers down and over its veined staff, strokin' it. My mind drifts: Hunter down on his knees, sucking me off, shaft moving in and out of his pretty and athletic mouth; Hunter kissing my nipples, the left one, the right one, the left one again; Hunter whispering into my mouth, holding my head to his chiseled face, "It's time to get busy on my oar, Galin … It's time to—

"You know the State Championship is coming up in a few weeks, Coach, and I thought … I thought maybe you could help me tomorrow morning … a private practice. If you can spare an hour of your time, I think I can use it."

I can still see him in my mind from the past Saturday, brown and adorable head bobbing up and down on his own meat; lips curling around rigger; sucking and slurping, groans filling the equipment shed along the Hudson; white gleaming spew jutting up onto the plane of his healthy well-developed chest—

"Coach Galin?"

"I'm right here." I let out a long sigh, ready to explode a burst of nightly goo onto my own shirt, carelessly decorating bare abs. "I'm thinking about it." My hand rocks up and down on my steel skiff. I pump my hips upwards, allowing the chair to creek madly underneath me, possibly echoing into the phone. I can't keep the load in—it's not possible. The overwhelming Hunter-pictures of sexual necessity that careen through my Reed-infested mind, and the infallible desires that build within my bliss-filled cock cause me to quiver in the chair, legs still propped on desk and widely spread, perspiration building on forehead, pumped arms working madly, wildly, and uproariously. There's no turning back to sanity and phone etiquette. No rhyme or reason occurs as my infatuation with the senior rower on the other end of the phone causes me to have an orgasmic rush. I can't take it anymore … *can't* … *won't*.

My breath grows to a heightened level as three liquidy strings of coach-glue shoots out of my polished scull and

157

glistens my lower torso's skin and bunched shirt. As the load adorns my chest I grunt prosaically into the receiver, "Tomorrow morning, Hunter ... Six o'clock at the equipment shed ... A private practice. Just you and me. No one else."

6:05 A.M.—he's not coming. Hunter Reed has blown me off. Fuck it, I'm gone, outta here. I'm about to head back to my 4-Runner when—for some unexplained reason—at the corner of my right eye I see something red and gold floating on the Hudson, escaping the early heated sun from the north. My attention is drawn to the spectacle almost at once. Out of nowhere comes a shirtless Hunter Reed in his slim rigger. The sleek and narrow two-man racing boat is being worked over by Hunter's masculine and bulky arms. His fisted hands span the aluminum sculling oars into the brown water, lifting them, allowing them to fall again, carrying out a beautifully constructed stroke that is championship-winning and breathtaking.

He sees me almost at once, directs the rigger to shore. I walk to edge of the river and look down into the rowing machine, compelled to lick my lips at the cut man with the still oars, desiring him, fending off a preconceived notion of becoming hard almost instantly by his mere presence.

"You getting in, Coach?" His dazzling, amethyst colored eyes shine in the morning light. Bubbles of perspiration dance across his forehead, along the arcs of his bulging shoulders, and down along the sculpted shell of his strapping torso.

Because I'm a coach, and have every right to be concerned with the senior's timeliness, I scold him in the rigger, "You're late!"

A smile to die for collects at the edges of his Italian lips. Reed heavily breathes, perhaps already exhausted by his morning activity. "I'm sorry ... lost track of time. I started early."

158

Of course he has started early; just like in the equipment shed a week before. I shake my head, "It doesn't cut it, Hunter ... Now let's rock and roll."

As I coach out orders to him, the fiberglass rigger careens through the water like fingertips over the supine silkiness of a freshly shaved chest. The built-in oars move magically with Hunter's keen abilities, continuously revolving up and down in mad circles. With Hunter positioned at the stern of the rigger, and me in the front, I call out, "Stroke! Stroke! Stroke!" as the boat glides majestically and quickly along the Hudson's murky current. My eyes concentrate on Hunter's position: biceps and arms toned just perfectly, moving in a rhythmical manner; feet locked against fiberglass braces; legs slightly spread with muscles bursting forth droplets of golden sweat; fists and fingers wrapped around rubber oar grips as if they are jock-cocks, working madly. I lick my lips uncontrollably as I see the rippled abs on Hunter's chest, parallel lines that are cruelly indented but deliciously nice. My mesmerized and intoxicating stare travels to the tight little naval lining his stomach and then to the V-area of his Viper sport shorts. The shorts, packing tightly to his mighty thighs, outline the seven soft inches of his promising jewel of the Hudson.

"What are you looking at?"

"Nothing," I respond rather quietly, suck in saliva, instantly ashamed at my unprofessional behavior.

"You're looking at my goods, Galin."

Is he smiling at me? Is Hunter finding this embarrassing moment for me amusing? "I wasn't. I was admiring your rowing technique. You're going to be fine in the championship."

Hunter chords, "You can't get enough of me, can you, Coach?"

I don't respond, because I *can't* respond, and *won't* respond, have utterly promised myself I won't become misled and viable to the young athletic and his strapping dude-needs or coach-cravings. Instead, I sit quietly, press my lips together, and fend off the burning and growing sensation of cock-birth in my too-tight shorts.

Something unexplained happens after rowing down the Hudson a mile or so in silence. Without instructions, the bulky senior navigates the rigger to shore along a set of windblown rocks and a backdrop of maple and birch trees, a secluded area in New York that is private and serenely perfect. With urgency, the head rower of the Nestleton College Rowing Team implores, "Time to get out of the boat, Galin … and put a stop to this uncomfortable state between us."

He's out of the rigger and standing in two feet of water, comes up to my side. I turn, peering into his wholesome manly eyes, and respond, "What uncomfortable state, Hunter?"

"My attraction to you … and your appetite for me."

"What are you …"

It's too late to speak. Hunter pulls at the back of my head, locks his mouth to mine, and causes me to feel overboard by his embracing kiss, causing me to break a professional rule, to melt, and to grow imperiously hard between my throbbing and needing to burst legs.

It's not right—but it's perfect. We are naked along the Hudson River in the shadowy privacy of the outdoors. Hunter Reed is hunched over a massive bolder as if he is stretching before a rowing event. He has his legs spread wide open and his head is dropped between them. He approaches the tippy-top sliver of his tongue to his own extension of Coach-pounder, and little by little he laps at the head of the oar, brushing it with his slippery man-tongue, teasing himself. Between his legs (silky looking balls and hardening cock drooping from this supine area) he catches my brown eyes with his amethyst ones, instructs me rather fluently, "Do your thing, Coach."

Of course, I oblige. Within seconds, I'm on my knees licking lips and mouthing the rower's skin on the nape of his back, rolling tongue down and over one butt-cheek, teasing his hole with condom-covered finger. With desire racing through my body, I position the tip of the saliva coated tongue against his skin, brush-stroking his flesh, listening to him suck and moan in an excited manner. My world spins around and around as if a cyclone consumes my body, lapping at Hunter's exterior, teasing and cajoling him, causing him to almost shoot his load all over the bolder. I'm not ready to screw him yet, although this seems to be what the senior champion desires—man pushing finger into ass, man lapping back-skin with greed. I merely become a mouth God behind him, tantalizing him by leaning forward, separating his ass cheeks with a delving and protruding appendage, meticulously harboring the digit into his boatlike shell, driving him mad and madder as he consumes his own cock-stem between slurping and noisy lips at work.

He can't bear the pleasure I provide, pulls off his own cock, whimpers in the tranquil and quickly sun-heated morning, "Galin ... Coach Galin, I didn't know you had it in you."

Hunter Reed's straight, mind you. But honestly, here's a man with his legs spread wide open for a chap's body parts to intrude, split him apart, tease his inner-most fiber with slippery niceness. Here is a man who has completely fallen for my immediate devices, lathering his hole with morning bliss, greed, and everything a college coach has always wanted.

The rower pulls away before he explodes a goo-rush onto the massive bolder. Hunter spins around with his eleven inches of fat slab in his right hand, informs rather rudimentary, "Do you want this, Coach?"

I still see him in the equipment shed from the week before: Hunter looks stinging and hot, rapturous in the splinters of morning light, delicious and spine-tingling. I have to have inside me, pounding and ravishing older me in his uncontrollable ways. I want to be nothing less than the remembered coach, for my long shaft, tight abs, and tight ass. For my—

As he fetches a condom from his left, behind rowing shorts near the rig, Hunter comments, "If I can't have you today, Galin … I'm afraid I will never have the opportunity again."

It melts me, yet my eight inch cock throbs mightily. I can't help myself anymore. I have to have him. It's now or never. I *can't* think of college rules, I *won't* think of college rules. Before I can understand logic, I'm hunched over like a young boy again, enjoy the movement of his plastic covered and pulsating shaft ripping into me, inch after inch, burning my insides as if it's an aluminum oar. Quickly, nonchalantly, and strummingly he hugs my hips with his immense palms, immediately banging my insides with his meaty, pounding and prodding contraption, mining my hole, digging for my inner-core with expected hunger. Minutes after minutes are shared with man inside man, the coach and his trophy-bearing athlete carrying out the beauty and romantic necessity between connected men. In and out he glides, the champion at work, practicing a win for a gold-awarding prize.

I become Hunter's mannish prey beneath him, Coach Galin spread open, choking on his favorite senior's cock from behind, squinting eyes, ready and willed to burst a creamy load alongside the flowing Hudson. There's absolutely nothing to prevent my bittersweet burst from flying out of my cockhead. If I don't pull off of Hunter's fiberglass-like structure, I'll come right here on the rock. With superhero speed I escape his pressing palms on my working hips, spin around, watch him rip off the condom from his chunky friend, as both of us begin to carry out what we know best, what rowers call … strokin' it.

His hands move quickly up and down on his rod. We stand facing each other, senior and instructor, demanding nothing less than a high-performance. He works his meat with skill and dignity, shares an arrogant smile with me, arches his neck and shows off its stricken cords, the modest

162

ripples lining his firm chest, flaunting the veins along his functioning shaft.

Both of us rock our splinters up and down, wildly racing in our own contest, breathing hard, glowing, flushing hands north and south with speed ... as if we are rowing.

"Stoke! Stroke! Stoke!" he calls out, becoming the coach.

I listen, watching him grin wildly, unable to pent his load anymore. I see his smile weaken and his eyes shine with a cultivated madness of lust. Fists move with rigger-speed as hips thrust forwards and backwards, forwards again ... as a morning drizzle of guy-gush daringly flies up and over his plane of skin, white sappy splotches decorating his rigid and flexing chest, glazing his body like icing.

It's too much to handle ... too mind-crazy ... too unreal.

"Blow it, dude! ... Blow it now!" Hunter demands, smiling over at me, flushing more sap out of his skull, garnishing his abs and nipples with steamy, outdoor goo.

As three, last incisive movements are carried out with perfection on his protein-slab, a white flood of coach-syrup nails my own chest and triceps, missing my mouth by only inches, spraying out of my meat-fixation. I jerk wildly, calling him: *defeater!, victor!, prize-winner!*

And, as the last droplets of guy-discharge leak from our still-hard paddles, it's Hunter who moves towards me, breathing chaotically with his chest rising and falling. The winner collects my mouth against his, an experienced kiss following, a kiss that will last throughout and beyond his graduation, and he finally whispers, "Now, I know why I've fallen for you, Galin."

WHAT A GUY WANTS

~ ~ ~

"We meet again, Alexandro," I say between the movements of his tongue dipping into my mouth, my back leaning against the bamboo wall of the restroom on the evening beach.

Taking in my shocking blue eyes, short tufts of mismanaged blonde hair, chiseled good looks, Alexandro Nadar responds in his heavy Spanish, "I wished summer break was every day, Tommy Pike." The Latino guide cups my hardening goods, causes me to feel elated and stiff, enticingly mesmerized that I have found him in Cancun— again.

Back in UCLA, I've missed Nadar's emerald colored eyes, dashing smile, and milk chocolate crew-cut, have returned to visit the hardening device in his tight khakis, prowling fingers over his eight inch goods. I've waited the longest year of my life for this: steeping boy-body with rippled muscles; extension of hard rod pressing against my stomach or insides; biceps slick with pure beach sweat; suntanned and Latino-dark skin next to mine during intoxicating sex. Isn't this what every guy wants? I have his meat-tube in my right hand and feel it's veins through the guide's cotton shorts. I say, "You haven't changed at all."

"Your *el pito* has gotten bigger, Pike."

"My what?"

He grabs my semi-hard cock in khaki shorts and begins to stroke it with his busy fingers, indulging it with new life. "It's bigger this year."

I begin to laugh at this, ready to have him go down on my meat right here and now, both of us knotted together outside the bamboo restroom, eating me whole, gagging on my length. But our concealed meeting in this social area is soon interrupted. Three Texas State dudes saunter up to the piss-palace. Abruptly, Nadar pulls his hand away from my rod and backs off from me, escaping. I'm left with my now pulsating rod bouncing between my hard legs, electrified and harder than hard, and immediately follow Alexandro's hot behind, deep into the Cancun wildlife.

Among palm trees and sand, half-hidden from intruders, Alexandro whispers into my ear, licking my skin with the tip of his tongue, "I know of a place where we can go for a reunion."

"I'm all yours, guy … Lead me astray."

There is complete silence between us as we scurry away from the beach and it's festive parties. Alexandro leads me to a narrow pathway that is lined with more palm trees and sand. I begin to see semi-dressed guys who are getting it on in the dim moonlight, somewhat hidden along the pathway. It's like an American park where boys pick up other boys and become heatedly entangled in sexual homo-positions. I see masculine shadows kissing and screwing, inflated cocks bending into tight boy-holes or hungry mouths. I hear moaning and crazy murmuring, "More … Give it to me more … Right there …" American dudes calling out into the night to their Latino lovers. And here, this mysterious place where I am feeling easy and unreal, an enchanting and mystifying place, the smell is rank but delicious, masculine sweat that is rich and arrogant, kind to my nose. Alexandro reaches for my hand, keeping me his, protecting me from a body snatcher that will use me for their ultimate harmony and hunger. I stay behind him for five hundred more feet, cautiously walk forward while listening to the sexual boys around me, feeling completely overwhelmed and enticed.

Eventually, we come to an opening at the end of the pathway. Bamboo poles are lit with fire, all of which are scattered around a regal and majestic lagoon the color of aqua-green. The light here shares a faint hue of yellow-gold brilliance, causing a variety of naked and masculine bodies to reflect with wholesome beauty along the lagoon's private beach. And in the distance, I see a waterfall on the opposite side of the lagoon where there are more unnamed and naked twinks holding each other, pressing their bare bodies together in promiscuous dances, tight and rippled torsos locked together, guys who are sexually entwined in unlimited positions. Moonlight shines into the blue-green pool of shimmering water where I view even more naked bodies (both American college students and Latinos) kissing and holding each other, swimming and fucking, some that are busy with foreplay and bucking wildly, while others stroke each other off with needed desires. Many of the dudes are in twosomes while others are in busy threesomes, connected together like puzzle pieces, groaning as they get licked or fucked, chanting to their Cancun sex god, enjoying this secret place that Alexandro Nadar shares with me.

"It's called *la orgia.*" I put the words together—group sex—and smile, holding Alexandro's right hand. He explains, "They have come to praise Macizo."

"Macizo?" I question.

"Our God of sex between chicos."

"In American we call it a boy-bar," I laugh, caressing Alexandro's solidly rippled chest, feeling the smooth skin of his torso, exploring the confined area of his taut nipples and ladder-like abs.

166

The tour guide leans into me, compresses his firm lips against my own, locks his hairless chest to my chest, and mysteriously responds in chunky English, "I think you're going to like it here, Pike."

We continue walking towards the lagoon, eventually kicking our sandals off along the sandy beach. Alexandro leans into me, breathes me in, consumes my musky aroma, and instructs, "I'm taking you in the lagoon with me." He peels the buttons free on my khakis, licks my left nipple, runs his tongue up along my chest, over my quivering neck, and eventually kisses my chin. The Latino god pulls my khakis away from my hips, pushes them off, and predicts in a soft tone that I find appealing, "Something tells me you're going to enjoy this." Now, he touches the firm piece of cock between my nervous legs, caressing ball-sack with straying fingers, sniffing one of my pits, consuming its salty flavor after lifting my arm, and enjoying the moment of mixing with this inexperienced *chico* from a busy place called California.

After he strips out of his khakis, dropping them to the sand, my eyes focus on the cut, eight inches of his shaft that stands upright and at attention. And like a good visitor on this romantic escapade, I move my right hand forward, touch his stem with three fingers, and play with his lagoon toy.

He moans with my stroking, saying something in eloquent Spanish that I do not understand. Alexandro becomes infatuated with my movements, clings to me, draws my body towards his and gently shoves his tongue into my mouth. Sealed together, an aromatic flavor of lagoon heat passing between us, our cocks press together, combine in a mutual tryst, and become harder by the transient seconds.

It is Alexandro who falls to his knees, the blue-green water rising up to his waist, his tongue moving southward against my body, crazily lapping at the tight abs that make up my stomach, lathering my naval with his pointed tongue, eventually finding the tip of my steeping erection, placing it into his mouth, falling and falling on its pulsing length, breathing me in, choking on the mass, sucking happily on the protein, causing me to feel infatuated, buzzing and wavering above him. I hold the back of his dark head, half-hypnotized by his hazel eyes, needing his mouth-movements, missing him. For the past year I have dreamed of this moment with him, find myself blessed and enriched with his oral pleasure, completely falling for this reunited passion that can easily be considered bliss.

He pulls off of my rod before I come in his mouth. On his knees, Alexandro looks up the plain of my chiseled chest and asks, "Will you swim to the waterfall with me?"

I nod my head, help him up, trust him, and follow Alexandro into the water until our narrow hips, pumped chests, and Hummer-wide shoulders are covered with the soothing water of this Cancun world. Together, like Neptune and Aqua-man, we swim to the other side of the lagoon where there are male vacationers by the amazing waterfall, sharing intricate means of sexual craving. Once surfacing I hear the guys moaning and groaning around me, sculpted bodies moving together in sexually adequate positions, mixing together in compromised behaviors. Here, in this other world, away from my hotel and luggage, a cultural difference than that in UCLA, I feel Alexandro against me again, lips connecting to my left shoulder and neck, taking me in, desiring my American skin, and inevitably falling for my blonde perfection. He says implicitly, "I have to taste you."

"Taste me?" I ask.

"Yes, taste you … Your skin is teasing me and I want more of you," he confirms, drawing me closer into shore, the tranquil water around our knees, and the waterfall directly behind us. In a gentlemanly manner he tells me to get on my knees in the water, that I'm very safe, and to spread my legs. I listen to him, facing a scene of three Latino jocks who are connected with mouths and cocks, orally satisfying their imperative needs, their dark bodies writhing together as a mutual and masculine hum vibrates through the lagoon because of their appealing delight.

168

He pries my ass open with two fingers, pressing their points against my pink hole, breaking me in. I feel the warm tip of his tongue lap at my man-sliver, pleasing me, turning me on, prompting my seven inches of hard shaft to pound and thump between my bent legs. Alexandro pivots his tongue inside me, holding my ass apart with his bare hands, slurping and groaning behind me, caressing my insides, allowing a pulsating vibration to spin wildly and triumphantly throughout my body. I become tranquil and at peace in front of him, his tongue probing and working my insides, his palms and fingers spreading my ass wide and wider, entering my hole, motivating me to moan with sexual hysterics, hungry for the guide's tongue-exploration. I murmur unexplainable things in front of him, watching the three jocks in the distance suck each other off, enjoying their festive and ripe embraces. I plead happily for him to stop before I spew in the lagoon, unable to keep my load from bursting.

Alexandro—still busy with his tongue-deeds, becoming quite mesmerized by my collapsible ass— negotiates his position behind me, eventually pulls away, crawls around and faces me, locks his puffed lips with my narrow ones, and says in Spanish, "You are meant to be with me, Pike. You are my Macizo."

It is here—a place that I could easily call Gay Utopia—in the warm Cancun water where we embrace, locking together with arms and legs, cocks teasing each other, tongues digging into the depths of slippery throats, bodies clinging together as the lighted bamboo poles flicker around the lagoon. We become like the others around us, overly aroused and preoccupied with each other's skins, observing and copying their sexual positions, listening to them as they chant and hum, groan and moan, coming together, spewing their sticky loads onto American or Latino skin, obeying their thirsts and hungers for each other at this magical and social playground where boys lust after other boys. We kiss each other hard. We pull apart. Alexandro whispers to me, "I want to have you in the waterfall now."

169

I reply quite fondly, adoring his emerald colored eyes, his perfectly molded body, his crew cut, and smile, "I am yours ... always," giving into the hardening sensation between my legs, and the appetite that I have gained for him.

Together—locked serenely, blissfully, and heatedly—both of us underneath the waterfall, I feel Alexandro Nadar behind me, pressing his hard goods against my tight ass, pivoting his palms against my legs as his arms wrap around my body. We stand under the heavy spray in the lagoon, desiring nothing less than each other in a full-fledged act of intimacy. Teasing me, he pulls away and slides a condom (a needed instrument that is somehow brought here from shore) over his steeping rod. Alexandro nibbles at one of my earlobes and murmurs helplessly, "Are you ready, American Pike?"

"Yes," I clearly respond, captivated by the moment. He hardly shares enough time for me to answer, though. Nadar pushes into me, breaking my buttocks open, holding me up at the same time with one of his palms wrapped around my muscled center. I'm hunched over with my fingers gripping kneecaps, half-standing and feeling his weight enter me, pushing my insides apart, his shaft having a secret reunion with my quivering chute. He thrusts his weight into me, all eight inches plummeting into my craving ass, causing me to whimper and digest his pole, choking in front of him with exhilaration and satisfaction as the waterfall luxuriously bathes our linked bodies.

"Me estas poniendo caliente," (You get me so hot.) he utters in the flowing water, pulsating inside me, rolling back and forth, clinging to my skin.

"You're worth the long wait, Alexandro." I chant in front of him with my eyes closed, half-delirious with a sensual and numbing awareness. The guide's hands grip my wobbling hips, one on each side, pulling me towards him, throttling his weight into every portion of my backside, convincing me that we have become believers in Macizo, pleasuring ourselves in His waterfall, feeding Him our sexual desires and heated lust. My body—a mere temple for Alexandro's use—feels paralyzed in his grip, anesthetized and warmly prosaic with his everlasting and hungry movements. And as the moments pass with our masculine tenderness, we become synchronized together, grinding and possessive of each other, relishing skin and ass and cock, desiring nothing less.

He hums behind me, "No pares nunca!" (Don't ever stop!) bucking me rowdily, calling out my name again and again within the falling water. Alexandro wraps a hand around my side, pinches a nipple, rolls fingers down and along my chest, finds my cock, and begins to move the skin on my college staff up and down, kindly and in an infatuated manner, needing no one but me—his American find.

It's too much ... I can't take it any longer. He's far too good for me, everything I have ever wanted. A god of sorts; a relic. My Latino friend and fan—discovered and all mine. I pull away from his fingers and off his pulsating and still packing rod that is in constant motion. I tell him in Spanish, "Let me touch you now," stepping behind him in the waterfall and having my seven inches of rod press against his dark buttocks. I reach around his solid chest with his back pressed against my nipples and abs, and apply my right palm to his shaft, immediately feeling warm skin that is veined and hard. The rod pulsates in my hand as I move its skin up and down, working Alexandro over. I hear him moan and groan in front of me, long and drawn out sounds that resemble chanting. He plunges my hand with his cock, rocking forward and backward, causing my own shaft to vibrate with mutual excitement. Positioned behind him, I toy with his cock and one nipple, my fingers busy with labor, my tongue working up the length of his neck, listening to him erupt with pleasure as he continuously calls out my name, needing to burst his load.

"Mas ... mas!" (More! ... More!) he blares into the fountain, bucking my hand, roaring with enthusiasm.

My fingers play with Alexandro's flesh, adoring him, finding him joyous and required for my Latino hunger. I pivot my fingers along his guy-beam, stroking it harder, prompting him to whine underneath the waterfall, wildly thrusting his hips forward, arching his neck, coming inside my palm and over my fingers, exploding sticky jism from his arched body in my arms, blowing the load with ease, practically crying in my grasp with erotic bliss, desiring no one else except for UCLA-me.

Breathing heavily, his cock still hard and upright like a flag, he pulls away from me and spins around, smiles at me, and says in pure English, "Your turn, Tommy Pike."

I can say nothing to him, locked to his eyes, enjoying his sculpted body under the aqua-blue water as he falls to his knees again, cupping his tight mouth over my goods, swallowing me whole, beginning to digest my meat with pure devotion, willing me to come. Alexandro's mouth moves on and off my protein, his fingers grazing the skin on my inner-thighs, sometimes toying with my balls, causing an everlasting state of euphoria to trap my body as I am left to do nothing more than swiftly jiggle in front of him, perhaps drowning under the waterfall's flow and his continuous sucking as he needs me to come. I breathe in and out, enthralled by this Cancun treasure, pulsating and trembling inside his mouth, practically unable to stand. I chant crazily, unable to store my load any longer, "Now ... I'm blowing now, Alexandro."

He pulls off my rod before I spew. My ooze sprays his plane of chest, which almost immediately washes away by the waterfall's flow. I watch dots of white sap decorate his neck and chest for mere seconds before the water cleans his skin. And on his knees, looking up at me, seeming somewhat dazzled and preoccupied with my existence, both of us spent, he runs his opened palms up and along my lateral chest that is very blonde. He is totally hypnotized by our movements together, muttering in heavy and awkward English, "You're what I want, Tommy ... Now let's do it again."

172

BE A MAN

~ ~ ~

Prey is this animal with natural instincts. He comes after me, tries to bite me, eat me whole, wants me so bad that he can smell me a block away, needing me, and desiring nothing less than me. And when the steamy Latino comes into my surroundings, obsessive of my skin, neurotic for a taste of me, he leans into my gymnast-shaped body and whispers in a sultry manner, "Have you ever been behind a man, Hush?"

I'm with other men at Rocket's Bar, a pool place located downtown with a nice lounge, frisky boys, and a dashing selection of naughty or nice dudes to choose from. I'm with Pete, Sloan, Malcolm, Terrance, and Dash, guys who protect teasing and straight-me from gay-invaders, and prevent me from becoming Prey's prey. I'm held back, surrounded, guarded, but still find an appealing magnetism for Prey. Underhandedly I create a way of slinking free from my boy-pack, close in on Prey's pumped body, and comfortably respond to his question, "What do you mean by *behind a man?*"

Springtime in Greenwich Village. A big storm circulates outside of Prey's bar. The lights flicker on and off as thunder booms overhead. Between booms, the six-plus dude laughs.

I laugh back.

Our eyes connect (Caribbean blue with his melting jade), blending, dancing, captivated.

"You're so sweet and innocent, Jacob Hush, that's what I like best about you."

Thunder again; this time louder. The lights flicker off, on, off again ... one second, two seconds—everyone's screaming and having a blast, unafraid ... on again. I lean into his ripped shoulder, take in a whiff of his bulky niceness, man-sweat that secretly makes me hard—a scent that pulls and drags me closer to his homo-exited-inflated world. Provocatively, I consume his maleness with ease and splendor, and whisper back in a convincing and conniving manner, "The only time I've ever been behind a man is in college, Prey, and that was playing football. How about you?"

"I don't fuck and tell," he charms me.

"I respect that."

"You'd better." He smiles, toying with me.

Lightening whizzes across the sky outside, crashes somewhere, makes me feel like Prey's taking a picture of my blonde, good looks. Thunder bangs again, two harmonious grinding sounds that reverberate together in the clouds. I'm unafraid, charmed by the storm, under its spell. Sweetly, I touch the hottie's square chin with two fingers, breathe in his emphatic bliss, become dazzled and dangerous by his testosterone flavor, and whisper into his slightly opened mouth, "How badly do you want me behind you, Prey?"

More lightening screams overhead; this time with thunder.

He smiles.

I smile back.

The lights go off for two seconds, click back on. Everyone's partying and dancing, uninhibited by the storm, possibly desiring its evening temper like a new club drug. Prey chants, "You're straight," slipping a hand down between charcoal colored chinos and an ab-covered stomach. He finds my drooping, hairless balls, and a friendly cock with droplets of pre-spew.

I pull my fingers down along the cords of his neck, between his P-town sized pecs, move the fingers and palm to a taut nipple, squeeze it generously, and respond, "I never said that."

"All the guys around here say you're straight."

He plays with my rod using busy fingers as a clap of thunder is followed by a zoom of lightning. The lights flicker in Rocket's again. Boys and Daddies cheer with spellbound glory at the storm's fury as I pinch the Latino's nipple again.

"All the guys around here don't know what they're talking about, Prey."

Prey licks the swelling cords on my neck.

I touch one of his tight abs under his dark tee.

"You a lonely guy, Hush?"

"Not when you're around."

Prey releases his hand from my chinos and consumes the Hush-spew from his fingers.

I pop a few more droplets into my pants and think I've become immortal.

"Tell me your secrets, Hush."

"Never," I whisper back.

We are so close. Our lips almost touch as heat forms between us and animal instincts develop. This is dangerous ground where man needs man. Our desires flare as Prey and Hush collide in an obstinate and steadfast manner, leaving both of us hard. We are about to kiss like men who are hungry for each other. Our worlds are about to collide within the hump and grind of Rocket's. I'm about to become Prey's meal when—

The kiss is terminated before I know it—we separate. There is the loudest cranking sound of thunder overhead. Lightning peels through the city as if Armageddon is beginning. Rocket's lights flash off, abruptly. A blanket of pitch black covers our bodies. I believe Pete, Sloane, Malcolm, Terrance, and Dash all come to my rescue, and pull me away from Prey, freeing me from the bar owner's masculine lair and sweet abduction.

A large hand grips my right palm, drags and steers me through the dark and sexy silhouettes of succulent bar-bodies. Night collects around the still-partying patrons as I feel hands on my taut ass, rigid chest, splay of back, and between my throbbing and somewhat nervous thighs. There are so many voices I cannot determine who's around me. I feel safe, though, being guided by the vat of men, navigated with precision and care. I wonder how many of the dudes I have kissed, held, or fucked. I wonder who is touching one of my tight little nipples, pinching it.

The noise of the crowd diminishes, though. I hear a door open and close as I'm being led deeper into the bar. There's no more thumping house rock, no more screaming and bantering queens in delight. Here in this separate part of Rocket's Bar, dark as night, fingers caressing the V-area between my legs, firming up my goods, the smell of Calvin Klein lingering around me, I hear Prey whisper into my right ear, practically licking my earlobe, "You're safe, Hush. You're in good hands."

"Of course I am," I whisper back. I begin to ask where we have meandered off to, but he blocks my words with an abrupt kiss, locking his mouth to mine, driving this slippery and heated tongue into the depths of my mouth, a rough attempt of suffocating me man-style. I feel Prey's fingers dance over my private parts, up the length of my chest, and then to the edge of my chin. Something smooth and firm rubs against my leg that I'm unfamiliar with. His other set of fingers dance over my back, holding me against him.

He pulls off sweetly, chants, "Do you want to be a hero this evening, Hush?"

Always! Who wouldn't? "Tell me how, Prey."

He laughs in the darkness, "Follow me downstairs."

"Downstairs?" I question. There must be a private, lighted room downstairs with daddies, leather, and an arrangement of naughty devices—something to hold my interest, of course.

Standing beside Prey I watch a flicker of lightning spark outside. Fresh yellow-white light fills the room. I see that we're in an office of sorts with a desk, papers, and chair. A flash of Prey's body shines: narrow chin, sculpted shoulders and chest, and stiff cock with drooping balls free of tight pants. Now I know what's been rubbing against my leg, teasing me. Quickly I giggle in a masculine manner, "Can I fill you in on a little secret, Prey?"

"What's that?"

"You've fallen out of your jeans."

"Have I now, Hush?" he asks while taking one of my palms and moving it in a leisurely manner to his throbbing and hard man-toys. Prey opens up my fingers as he nibbles at my neck, breathes my untamable skin into his lungs, and gently begins to tease his firm property with my hand. Challenging a kiss from me, he pulls away from my neck and asks, "Now tell me how that happened?"

I feel the veins in his eight inches of pounding plaything. The stiff slab is uncut and muscled. Fingers find a triangle shape of pubic hair and two fuzzy balls. Inside the dark office I hear Prey moan beside me, enjoying my hand-tour, relishing our private moment together as more thunder spins and streaks through the city's sky. Prey melts beside me, captivated by my handy gestures, obeying their gentle strokes and teasing. He grunts in a pleasant manner, "Why do you make me chase you, Hush?"

I kiss his mouth and neck, the niceness of his chin, gradually pull off and respond, "Because you deserve nothing less."

"A man's hunt?" he questions.

"Exactly," I respond, moving my palm and fingers up and down on his shaft, exploring his flesh and balls, the beauty of this night-game between heated males.

"You're straight?" he questions again.

"Of course I am," I respond.

177

"Then what are you doing right now?"

"Man-handling you, Prey. Like you've always wanted me to do."

My words cause a spurt of creamy, white goo to leak out of his dude-pistol. The cream runs down the veins of his cock and onto my fingers. Because I have always wanted this to happen (a hidden desire that is most unexposed), and because I have always wondered what another guy's sap tastes like (a deep-seeded craving of guy lust that penetrates my soul and burning crotch), I move the fingers off his rod and place them against my lips. Gently I lap off his blow with my pointed tongue, carefully and longingly.

Another spark of lightning infiltrates the room like a camera's flash. Prey sees my exhibition and asks, "Do you like the taste of it, Hush?"

It's bitter and sweet and just right. "I need more," I murmur, craving the bar owner and his mysterious ways, desiring nothing less than his sculpted body against my own ... *secretly*.

Abruptly he pulls away, tugs up his jeans, zips his zipper, and adds, "There's much more. You have to be a hero first, though, okay?"

"You're playing games with me, aren't you?"

Our mouths are so close we can merely lick each other. I believe our eyes lock together in the thick darkness, reading each other, trying to convey some type of lateral authenticity to the moment, a lingering of sorts that prompts a useful seduction between stinging men. He chides romantically while brushing fingers up along the delicate curve of my back, "My intuition tells me that you like playing guy-games, Hush."

I smile in the shadows and respond, "It's time you show me how to be a hero, okay?"

At the top of a tunnel-like structure in the gloomy blackness—a stairwell, I presume cynically—Prey instructs, "Slip your hands into my back pockets and follow me."

I prefer the touch of his ass: tight, firm, and bulbous. I listen to his helpful and alluring command. Incisively my fingers slip against his curved rump that I long to peel out of denim and lick succulently until death do us part. And for the very first time in my conceivably *straight* life, my mind wonders off to his bedroom, against the bar or back wall, anywhere where we can be committed to each other with expounding sincerity of man indulging man, bonded by the needs of impure and naughty sex, passionate kissing, and a parallel compatibility.

Slowly we walk into a pit of charcoal light, step after step. In front of me, Prey says, "Be careful."

"I'm right behind you."

He laughs, "I hope so."

"I'm not going anywhere."

Our footsteps are quick and falling as we make our decline into the basement of Prey's bar. At the bottom, more dark here, very cramped, a plateau of wooden boards and men, he stops abruptly in front of me. Accidentally I bump into his ass, cock meeting denim, stinging for life and a man-cure.

He says, "You found me."

"I didn't have to go very far."

He turns around and takes me into his hulking arms. As Prey holds me, he murmurs, "I have to turn your breaker on now."

"My breaker?"

He moves one palm away from my side for a second. I hear a *pop!* and *click!* The lights turn on. Blasts of cheering patrons howl overhead and house rock begins again. The place is back to thumping.

We see each other and smile in the new light. Prey pulls his playful hand away from the breaker and immediately cups my crotch—my own electrical device—and begins to rub it with a soothing action. He says in a derelict's manner, "Have I turned you on yet?"

"When you first found me a few weeks ago."

179

There is too much energy between us, a highly combustible fusion of man-desire lingering and connecting us together. I realize quite plainly that it is here in the obscurity at the bottom of the steps that we are meant to be together: sculpted man indulging homo-skin, chests and nipples touching, steeping shafts kissing. It is inevitable—we will digest each other on this dark and stormy night with vibrations overhead and loud music, with a bar full of the hottest guys on the planet, but not as steamy or rock-hard and good looking as Prey. We will act like heated lovers or mating animals in springtime. Lust is binding. Sex is our cure and indulgence. One conceivably straight man will connect to a gay one, both mixing, combined, and molded. This little adventure in the dark will turn into something magical and everlasting. A fulfillment of two men entwining as one. Prey will find his flesh-dream with me and carry it out with pure, masculine delight, with greed and skill, devouring every part of my skin, tasting my everlasting straight-juice until there is not a single drop to be craved.

And I—breathlessly, hypnotically, eagerly— will pursue a homo-erotic pathway of desire out of mere curiosity, out of inquisitive need, perhaps using him in all the right ways, a man on a mission in the dark, finding a rhythmic and pulsing sensation of sex between men for the first time. Our lives will join intimately and intentionally. I hunger for him like no other man in my masculine world. He is electric, leaving me stunned and astonished by his body and words. Prey is vigor and energy. Found.

"You're perfect for me, Hush."

Our eyes hang together in a sweet manner. "I don't understand."

He smiles, "To break me in, of course." He reaches between my legs again and gently squeezes my nine-inch pounder. "You're perfect for riding my ass … giving me what I want and need."

The rest is an utter blur. Thunder roars and lightning cracks above the Village. Prey becomes an essential pill by locking his lips to mine. He holds my hips, rubs his chest to mine, grinds me, dry-humps me, cups me close and closer to him. Eventually he pulls off of my lips and whispers something like: "I can't take any more of you like this," and strips my shirt off, sucks on one firm nipples with rushed and intense lips, and runs a hand up and down the center of my nicely carved chest, fingering abs with delectable proficiency. He rolls his narrow and slick tongue down the ladder of rippled niceness, breathing heavily, concentrating on his find. The Latino laps at the blonde fuzz beneath my naval, fingers my chinos loose, unzips my goods, finds no boxers, and …

"What are you doing?" I ask above him, inside his mouth, feeling dizzy and woozy and unreal and majestic.

Prey is far too busy to answer. He slurps up one inch after the next of my plump fixation, adoring his keep, savoring my pumped rod. He ingests all nine inches of my swelled cock, each inch slipping deeper and deeper into his throat, feeding himself. The dude is hungrily bemused and completely hypnotized by rumored, straight cock.

It is mere heaven above him as music thumps in my eardrums and I begin to pump his ravenous mouth. The basement swirls around me: cases of beer, brooms, and boxes of unused toiletries. As I hold onto his shoulders, balancing myself, Prey eats me up whole, gagging on my equipment, fingering my chest, pinching nipples or grazing neck cords, driving me mad and madder above him, leaving me paralyzed in his mouthy embrace.

Before pre-ooze shoots out of my dashing spigot, squirting a few droplets onto the boards where we begin to spoil each other's skin, Latino Prey pulls off and away. He quickly wipes the back of his hand across my face and gallantly chimes, "Nice breaker, dude."

Prey cannot keep his pants on; he's far too excited about our secretive and impromptu rendezvous. Hurriedly he peels away black tee and shows off caramel colored skin,

181

chunky pecs, and dark specs of masculine hair along the muscular curve on his exemplary chest. He stands looking at me with his jade colored eyes, studying and analyzing me as he pulls innocent-white boxer briefs down to his knees, stunning me into a dazzled phase of absolute silence.

"You like what you see, don't you?"

As the storm still rakes and rocks over the city I melt before him, awestruck and cannibalistic, unable to fend myself from bending down on my knees and groping his eight inches of husky tube in both hands. Once positioned in front him, staring up the plane of his Peruvian chest, I respond to his question by leaning forward and lapping at the brown head of his smooth and solid cock.

He is experienced and rides my mouth and canal-like throat with his pulsating eight inches, ripping into me, pressing hands to the back of my head, pushing me into him, causing me to gag in a harmonious manner with the plundering storm. I choke and gasp for air, pleased by our actions, eating him whole, bathing him with saliva and warmth. Prey breathes heavily in the heavens, thrusting hips forward, pounding my face and lips, wobbling and tottering with my succulent and sucking action. The guy burns for a need to come in my mouth, cleansing me with his fiery load of hot and sappy jizm, energized to blow a discharge on my skin, washing me clean of my guy-innocence—forever.

"No more, Jacob … No more," he confesses, pulling out of me and pushing me away at the same time. "I want to save this treat for you." Speedily he steps out of shoes and jeans, runs his lips over mine, and instructs, "Get behind me now … I can't wait any longer … *Please.*"

My friends (Pete, Sloan, Malcolm, Terrance, and Dash) cannot save me—because I wish not to be saved from Prey. There is nothing gay about my performance as I slip behind the man, positioning my hands against his firm hips. Slowly I rub my extension of Hot Rod-covered shaft against his tightly spread hole, teasing him, listening to Prey half-whimper in front of me in his mediocre, Spanish accent, begging for more action.

Lights flicker on and off in the basement like a discothèque. It's a total turn-on for me as inch after inch of my driver opens Prey up and navigates his hole. The feeling of his skin wrapped around my pole is exhilarating. Tight flesh collapses against my stake as it feeds into him, spreading him wide and wider, pushing into the Latino with gay necessity, choking him with my cock, pressing fingers into his hips as thunder booms outside. I recite wildly to him, "Isn't this what you want, Prey? Isn't this what you were talking about earlier this evening?"

He is mad for me and the post that splits him into two pieces. Prey groggily eases forward and backward, riding my meat, pleased with my position. I leave him captivated and driven as his tight sliver of ass spreads open for me, collapsing rod inside him, pulling out, pushing in … again and again and again.

"More," he moans with perseverance. "Give it to me, Hush … More!"

This is what he needs … this is what he wants, desires, and has been craving for the longest of weeks. Finally, I am behind the man of my delusional dreams, becoming captivated by our motion in the basement, completely overwhelmed with our movements of to and fro, pounding his packed ass with everything I have to offer him. Our actions are unyielding and fiery, passion between straight and gay men—an imprisonment of sexual cure for the both of us, electricity.

He and the storm are enigmatic as I blast the inches into him, pull out, push in again. He screams in front of me as balls slap vigorously and rapturously against his backside. Prey becomes my ultimate toy as my heroic advancements increase, allowing me to scream at the top of my lungs, willing to blow a warm and creamy load into the condom, unable to hold back.

He hollers, "Hush! Hush!" as he rides me like an experienced Latino lover.

Suddenly I can't take it anymore. I'm too energetic and heated, too stimulated. I pull out of him and release the condom, spin him around. He watches me blast atomic and bursting arcs towards him, hands plowing meat, fists working hard.

"Wash me down, dude. This is what I've waited for."

My white and gluey load drips from his lats and abs to his thighs and cock, decorating him in the night, marking his skin with hetero-spew for the first time.

"You're turn now."

He listens. Prey jacks his meat up and down with a steady and ultimate passion that is unbelievable. Hands work like well-oiled machines. His eyes connect to the plain of my chest as I stand in front of the breaker box. He aims directly at the center of my chest, and attempts to target my skin with his sappy load. And with urgency he groans, mesmerized by the moment with me, fixated to our exploited accomplishments, relishing my acceptance of him. Prey begins to spray his load out of his electrical tool with ease, fascination, and enthrallment.

He misses my chest, though—an error at hand. Hot, fiery goo flies over my right shoulder, spray after spray, and hisses in the breaker box. Sparks fly as his orgasm rockets. Smoke rises in a tiny cloud as a bolt of energy leashes through his body, causing him to become spent.

I laugh with excitement, "Now you're a hero, Prey," sarcastically.

He hugs me as the lights go out in Rocket's Bar because of his miscalculation. Prey connects our chests together. Romantically, lightning and thunder zooms above the city as the owner's spew sizzles in the breaker box. There's no apparent fire except for what I'm feeling in my soul, I know. It's Prey who cups and keeps me in his arms, our slick chests touching, lips very close. He whispers, "Have you fallen for me, Hush?"

Before kissing him like a boyfriend in the darkness, a meant-to-be kiss that I will never forget, giving into my clandestine and enigmatic desires, I whisper back, "Yes ... I think I have."

About the Author

R. W. Clinger travels between Pittsburgh and Florida. His hobbies include men-watching, boy-bar hopping and beachcombing. His novellas include *The Weekender*, *Sting Like a Bee*, and *Splash Boys*. R. W. is currently at work on a new gay novel. A few more of his works include

The Pool Boy
Astray
Monster
Rough
Four Men
Chapman's Tools
College Guys at Play
What He Wants
Something to Go Away With
Study Him
The Underside of Life
Guy-Time

Made in the USA
Coppell, TX
28 November 2024

41219491R10109